A.B. Church

Measure for Measure

A Novel. Vol. 3

A.B. Church

Measure for Measure
A Novel. Vol. 3

ISBN/EAN: 9783337101145

Printed in Europe, USA, Canada, Australia, Japan

Cover: Foto ©Andreas Hilbeck / pixelio.de

More available books at **www.hansebooks.com**

MEASURE FOR MEASURE.

A NOVEL.

BY

THE AUTHOR OF

"GREYMORE."

" Who shall win my lady fair?
  .   .   .   .   .   .
The bravest man, that best love can,
Shall win my lady fair."
Madrigal.

IN THREE VOLUMES.

VOL. III.

LONDON:
HURST AND BLACKETT, PUBLISHERS,
SUCCESSORS TO HENRY COLBURN,
13, GREAT MARLBOROUGH STREET.
1862.
The right of Translation is reserved.

MEASURE FOR MEASURE.

CHAPTER I.

A NOVEMBER AFTERNOON.

"I SHALL be obliged to go to London again soon," said Stephen Menteith, one morning at breakfast, a few days after the dinner party. "It is very provoking, when I am anxious to stay here as much as possible."

No answer was made; Mr. Clyde went on eating his breakfast, and Beatrice turned over the leaves of a newspaper. Her only sensation was one of relief—to be free from the restraint of Stephen's presence, even for a few days, was worth something.

"Mrs. Clyde was speaking of going to

town for a short time," continued Stephen, turning to Beatrice—"it might suit her to go now."

"I never heard that mamma had any decided idea of going," said Beatrice. "She cannot find any pleasure there at this season."

"It was on your business she intended going," said Stephen, in a lower tone.

"My business is not very pressing," said Beatrice, colouring a little; "and does not require a journey to London."

"It cannot be put off very long," said Mr. Menteith, emphatically. "I must leave England in December, and, of course, I wish to take my wife with me," he added in a whisper.

"Papa—some more coffee?" asked Beatrice.

"No, thank you, child—I have finished" —and, more in accordance with Stephen's wishes than with those of his daughter, he rose and quitted the room.

"We must come to some arrangement,"

said Stephen, when he and Beatrice were left alone. "It is customary, I believe, for the lady to fix the wedding-day, and I wait now for you to fix yours. You cannot delay it beyond the end of November."

"And you are quite resolved to take me back to Rio with you?" said Beatrice, with a rather faltering voice.

"Quite—I will never trust you out of my sight again," said Stephen, vehemently—"it is unreasonable to expect anything else. I came to England, intending to take you back with me, and then I had not half the inducement I have now."

"But, as you say you do not care to have a wife who does not love you, surely you need not be so anxious to keep her with you."

"You do not know what you are saying. I will secure you, at any rate—I will trust to making you love me afterwards. No—I will never expose myself to the torment of imagining you may yet——"

Stephen stopped abruptly.

"Well," said Beatrice, after a pause, and speaking with effort—" as I am already your wife, I suppose you have authority in all things. You command me to fix the day for the second ceremony to be gone through—a wicked mockery, it seems to me —however, I have no power to contend against circumstances, and I may as well say this day month."

"Thank you," said Stephen. "That will be the 29th of November—you have gone to the utmost limit—however, I will not press you. And you are my wife now, are you not?" he continued, looking at her eagerly and fondly—" say so again; I like to hear the sound."

"Since you know that I am your wife, and have no power to free myself, the mere sound of the word can hardly signify," said Beatrice.

"It brings the reality more before me— if you loved as I love you would understand —it is real, is it not?"

Stephen spoke with unusual impetuosity, and seized her hands wildly. It seemed as if he required some perpetual assurance that she actually belonged to him.

"It is no use repeating what you know to be a fact," said Beatrice; "and you must let me go—I have not seen mamma yet this morning."

Stephen released her hands slowly, looking earnestly and sadly into her face.

"I will not keep you—and it is only a month," he said half to himself. "Stay," he added, as she was leaving the room, "perhaps you will tell Mrs. Clyde that I must go to town in two or three days—she may be able to arrange for your visit at the same time."

"I have no wish to go myself," said Beatrice—"you must speak to mamma yourself."

"They shall go," said Stephen to himself, when she had left him; "I will not lose sight of her during this month—it seems to me sometimes as if she would escape me yet."

He carried his point about the London journey. Mrs. Clyde, when once she had become reconciled to the idea of having Stephen Menteith for a son-in-law, threw herself with the utmost ardour into the preparations for the wedding, and did not believe that Beatrice could have a fitting trousseau unless they both went to London to superintend the details of it.

Beatrice's indifference to her personal adornment provoked her, and the night before the journey she reproached her for her want of interest.

" You let everything fall upon me, Beatrice," she said; "if you were to be dressed like a Hottentot, I don't believe you would mind. And it is very hard upon me, so much pleasure as I have always taken in your beauty, to have you looking a fright upon your wedding-day, and knowing that when you are gone you will not care a straw how you look."

"Dear mamma, I am sure you and Larkins will prevent my looking a fright, and afterwards what does it signify? Besides, you may depend upon it that feminine vanity will last with me as long as any other sensation; and when I have no one else to trust to, I shall take pains to make the best of myself."

"But you look so dismal—upon my word, you will lose your beauty if you don't take care; and it is so distressing to see you."

"Mamma, how can I be cheerful? You know what reason I have for being miserable."

"It would not be so bad if you would see things in a reasonable light. Mr. Menteith may not be the man you would have chosen, but he is nothing to be ashamed of now. He is plain certainly, but his manners are good, and he is in an excellent position at Rio. It is a hard trial to part with you, but it is a consolation to know that you will

take a lead where you are going—and in a
few years you may return, and——"

"Pray do not follow the course of my
life further, mamma. I will try to endure
my lot with patience—more I cannot promise, when everything that is bright and
worth living for is torn out of my existence."
And Beatrice escaped to her own room.
She was even more wretched than usual, on
this her last night at home: when she returned, her wedding-day would be so near—
it seemed almost as if she were now bidding
farewell to the faint shadow of liberty that
remained to her.

And then the preparations!—how she
loathed them!—they brought before her so
much more palpably the deceit in which
she had been living for the last eight years.
She—in reality a married woman—was
supposed to be absorbed in the details of
bridal costume—she was to be looked upon,
by milliners and dressmakers, as a *fiançée*,
on whom they were to exercise their skill,

in order that she might appear a splendid
bride—she was to go through a solemn
ceremony, which had, in truth, no meaning
for her—she was to desecrate a holy place
by vows which she could not utter in sin-
cerity—vows which could not bind her
more securely than she had been already
bound for long years by the laws of her
country—vows which she had broken.

For the first time, complete horror of
the way in which she had acted and felt
came down upon Beatrice, almost crushing
her under the sense of her guilt. True,
circumstances had entangled her in a web of
falsity, which she had not, of herself, force
to break—she had been compelled to appear
in society as a disengaged girl, and men had
been at liberty to look upon her as one
whom they might love; but these very circumstances should have made her more
guarded; at the risk of seeming proud and
cold, she should have held herself distant
and aloof—no man ought to have been able

to speak to her as Captain Denbigh had
done.

Burning blushes crimsoned her cheeks as
she thought of the past, and sincere peni-
tence smote her heart for the deep deception she had practised, the sorrow she had
caused.   But since that time had she never
erred in a like manner? Ah! between
that period and this there had been an era
of which Beatrice dared not think, and yet
the contemplation of which allured her
with almost irresistible fascination.

Lionel Constable had loved her, and she,
too, for some brief, entrancing moments,
had felt the intoxicating joy of love.   Even
now her brain swam with delight, and an
ecstatic thrill ran through her, as she remembered how the cup of bliss had been
held to her lips—how for one rich, life-
filled minute she had dared to taste it.
But bitter shame and intense self-reproach
atoned immediately for the short transport,
the dangerous remembrance of a forbidden

happiness. If Lionel knew the truth, how he would despise her! That she, who ought to have withdrawn herself vigorously from him, had encouraged and piqued him—suffered him to declare his love—nay, more than that, to read in her eyes the humiliating confession that she loved him! She in whom love was sin, unless felt for the man she loathed! She whom it was sin to love!

Sin, for him—for Lionel, the pure, generous, chivalrous—the man of all others highest in her estimation. No! it could not be—he was unconscious, innocent of the evil—he had believed her free—he was still good and noble—he had not erred—*she* alone was guilty, but alas! not alone miserable.

She had blighted him—such love as his could not be easily rooted out—it would long endure, poisoning the wholesome spring of existence that had been so strong and bright within him.

She who had dared to love him had done this—desiring to grasp delights which her fate forbade her, she had condemned him to wretchedness.

Her pleasure-loving nature had first prompted her—then a reckless, passionate snatching at momentary joy had urged her on, until she had brought him and herself to the verge of despair.

Oh! that blind striving against her lot! Oh! that rebellion against the inevitable! Oh! for the past to return!

How differently she would have acted! How she should have struggled for patient submission, for meek endurance of the evil which the force of circumstances, and her own girlish rashness, had brought upon her! How she should have endeavoured to look upon her misery as only the fitting consequence of the deed which, though partly forced upon her, need never have been committed, had not exaggerated, self-conceited ideas of grand devotion, mistaken notions of filial duty, reconciled her to its accomplishment. Beatrice could see now, by the light of intense suffering, the whole madness and error of her life during the last eight years. First she had bound herself to be the wife of a man whom she could only fear and dislike—then, when visions of happiness had burst upon her, as life opened before her, she had fretted under the yoke, had grown bitter and scornful, despising those who enjoyed what she could never hope to possess—and then, goaded by what she saw around her, impelled by a blind longing for happiness, she had "caught at shadows," falling at length under the enchantment of a love which must be crushed within her, and the very remembrance of it wiped out of her heart as an evil stain.

The immediate result of her meditations showed itself in a slight decrease of the contemptuous manner in which, when not under the influence of fear—the fear chiefly of causing an outbreak between him and Lionel—she had treated Mr. Menteith.

During the time they spent together in London she behaved to him with indifference rather than repugnance, yet there was nothing in her demeanour likely to delude him into the idea that he would ever inspire her with a warmer sentiment.

Only very strong love, and a high opinion of his peculiar powers, could have kept alive in him the hope that, when Beatrice was once alone with him, away from all former friends and associations, he should be able to infuse into her some of the depth and intensity of his own emotions.

He was not very much with her in London, after all, for he and Mr. Clyde had business to attend to, and Beatrice and her mother were in a whirl of shopping, so that they rarely met till evening.

Beatrice went about like a victim—and, indeed, she might literally be said to be one—preparing for sacrifice. Her mother's interest in all matters connected with her adornment, and even with her future comfort, could not fail to be trying to her, and she underwent repeated tortures from such speeches as the following, which brought before her in vivid clearness the future misery of her daily life:

"I have just been ordering some of the loveliest thin muslin dressing-gowns for you, Beatrice; all trimmed with work and ribbon —you know in that hot climate they will be so nice to come down to breakfast in— and you need not dress till later in the day —and I suppose it will be as Mrs. Forsyth tells me it is in India, the ladies will dress a good deal for the evening drive. I have told Madame Dévy where you are going, and she is to let you have a set of tulle bonnets, all equally light, but differently trimmed. Mr. Menteith seems to admire you in a hat, so we must look out for some pretty riding-hats. I think one of them

might have a long, white ostrich feather, it
would suit your dark hair, &c. &c."

One afternoon, when Beatrice was thoroughly worn out, after spending a morning
in trying on dresses and choosing wreaths,
she felt strongly inclined for the refresh-
ment of air and exercise.   Her mother was
lying down, her father and Mr. Menteith were
in the City, so her time was her own, and
as the lodgings the Clydes always occupied
during their visits to town were in the
neighbourhood of Kensington Gardens, she
resolved to turn her steps thither, and take
a solitary stroll.

Her mother perhaps, had she known,
might have insisted upon the propriety of
her taking an attendant with her, but
Beatrice's notions were too independent for
her to feel any alarm, or see anything
unfitting, in walking by herself.   She was,
in truth, pining for air and freedom; in
the country, in the midst of all her tortures,
she could obtain a little distraction and

fictitious excitement, riding at a wild pace over hill and dale, or taking scrambling walks in woods and lanes; but here, in dreary London, there was nothing to make her forget herself, or to stir the animal buoyancy of spirit which was even yet too strong within her to be utterly quenched. Nothing on this dim November afternoon could rouse her from the indifferent languor into which she seemed, for the present, to have fallen. She walked listlessly along, crushing occasionally a dead leaf beneath her feet, and feeling, even as she did so, the depressing influence of autumn weigh more heavily upon her soul—glancing up, now and then, through the interlacing, well-nigh leafless branches at the grey sky, gloomy as her reflections—and gazing sometimes, across the gathering mist, at the faint outlines of buildings looming out in the distance, indicating the existence of that busy world where the noise and tumult of life were hurrying on—where

there must be brains as weary as hers,
hopes as withered, hearts as seared and
dead.

Dead! Was hers a dead heart?—was the
rush of sudden joy, the whirl of countless
conflicting sensations, the mad quickening
of pulse, the dance of blood through every
vein, significant of death?—the tumult of
hope, despair, yearning, rapture, agony,
which racked her inmost soul, as a turn in
the path brought within her sight the man
for whom her eyes had pined and her heart
grown weary, even whilst schooling herself
to dread his presence, and to shrink from
his memory—Lionel Constable—did all
these feelings belong to one in whom the
vital spring was crushed and broken?

The first moment of meeting brought joy
to both; but joy so involuntarily indulged,
so ruthlessly checked, that surely it might
be deemed blameless. To bow and pass on
would have been impossible—to speak and
not say more than common words of civility

would have been equally so. Chance had brought them together, and though nothing but misery could ensue from the encounter, Lionel felt that it must not pass without some slight explanation between them. He had ascertained so much, that he must ascertain more — must learn, if possible, from Beatrice's own lips the cause that had made her bind herself for life to the man who was so unlikely ever to have been her choice. He turned round and walked by her side, but how they fell into conversation neither of them exactly knew. The words exchanged were not many, and not conventional. In a short time, and in plain, strong language, Lionel made Beatrice aware that he knew she was married.

The shock was so great—the consciousness that he knew the gulf between them, and must scorn her for falsehood and weakness, was so overwhelming that Beatrice could not speak. Lionel's eyes, full of severity, seemed scorching the very depths of her

soul, reading her every thought, probing
and burning into the inmost recesses of her
conscience, reproaching her with the stern-
ness of his innocence, and with her own
guilt.   At last she said—

"You know the truth now, and I feel that
you must despise me.   I have no excuse to
offer, except that I was compelled to act a
part, and that it was difficult, without telling
the whole, to make it evident that I was not
free.   I was greatly to blame, but I could
not help the whole.   If I have given you
pain—and I feel that I have done so—forgive me!"

"Forgive you!" said Lionel, and his
voice, full of a rare tenderness, sank into
Beatrice's heart with healing power.   But
he checked himself suddenly—he durst not
be tender, or his impulses might have
mastered him, and he could not have answered for his future and hers.

"There is one thing I wish to ask you,"
he said, in calm, measured tones.   "When

you bound yourself, eight years ago, you must have been very young—did you act by your own free-will, or were you led by others?"

"I consented of my own free-will," said Beatrice; "but there were inducements which I cannot explain. Had I been older, I would not have acted in the same way."

"And those inducements—may I ask about them?"

"No—no—I cannot explain—I dare not tell you. I have said too much already. The thing is irrevocable."

"I know that full well," said Lionel, sadly; "from the moment when these two names, Stephen Menteith and Beatrice Clyde, struck my eyes in the Register Book of St. Benedict's district, they have been present to my mind. But one thing more —from that time, until Mr. Menteith's arrival in England this year you had not met?"

"Never," said Beatrice. "From that morning, the seventh of September, eighteen hundred and fifty——, when the ceremony was performed, I never saw Mr. Menteith until he returned from Rio, the evening after our pic-nic at Glendale. It was understood all the time that we were to appear unmarried before the world, and go through a second ceremony afterwards."

Lionel had started at Beatrice's mention of the date, and seemed lost in thought during the rest of her sentence.

"Seventh of September, did you say?" he asked, eagerly.

"Yes; I cannot easily forget the date."

"Strange!" exclaimed Lionel, after musing a little; "I could have sworn that the date in the book was the sixth."

"I am quite positive that the seventh was the day," said Beatrice.

Lionel's face brightened, and then grew thoughtful again, whilst Beatrice watched him with increasing interest.

"I cannot be mistaken," he said, at length, "I can see plainly the book before me, with the row of dates—1st, 2nd, 3rd, 4th, 5th, 6th—and there my search ended— opposite that date, in letters that seemed fire, I read your names. Are you convinced?—have you anything to support your idea that it was the seventh?"

"No," said Beatrice; "but I am convinced in my own mind—how could I be mistaken about the most momentous transaction of my life? Do you think I have not noticed, in spite of myself, every anniversary of that day—each more bitter than the last? But I should not speak in this way"—she paused, but presently added,

"I have a record, too—I had forgotten— an old diary, in which the date is written."

"Would you mind showing me the diary? I do not wish to be meddling or impertinent, but to satisfy my own mind, I should like to be certain that the date was the same as that in the Register."

"I would show it you," said Beatrice, "if
I had it here, but I left it at Wynthorpe."

"Then send me the leaf out of it, when
you return home," said Lionel, eagerly; "I
must compare the dates."

"But if the dates were not the same,
would it make any difference?" said Beatrice, a wild gleam of hope rising in her
eyes.   Lionel saw her look, and a profound
pity filled him—he durst not let her hope,
where such slight grounds for hope existed.
He might catch at a bare possibility himself,
a vague idea of some essential mistake, but
he durst not let her trust to anything so
intngaible.   So putting on an air of grave
composure, he answered,

"Scarcely, I imagine.   But just to satisfy
my curiosity, to ascertain whether or not
my memory has played me false, I hope
you will allow me to see the diary.   Are
you leaving town shortly?"

"We intend to go the day after to-morrow," said Beatrice.

"Then you will send the leaf containing the date immediately?"

"I am afraid—I don't know whether I ought," began Beatrice, but Lionel interrupted her.

"There can be no harm in it. The peculiarity of our thinkings of two different dates strikes me, and I should like to know which of us is right. I do not ask for a single line, remember—only inclose the paper in an envelope, and I shall be satisfied. Here is my address," and he gave her a pencilled scrap from his pocket-book.

"I will do it," said Beatrice; "and now you must leave me—I am near home, and it is better to part at once."

"I will not ask to stay longer with you," said Lionel; "but we may shake hands as friends, surely?"

"If you wish it, after all I have done," said Beatrice, and she held out her hand.

Yet it was not merely as a friend that Lionel clasped it. Wisdom, honour, prudence, were all forgotten in the instant that their palms met; both hearts were beating alike with love and agony; then suddenly, as with a mighty effort, the hands were torn asunder, and Beatrice and Lionel pursued their separate ways.

CHAPTER II.

A LEAF OUT OF AN OLD DIARY.

LIONEL spent the next few days in a state of torturing suspense, but on the fourth morning after the day of his meeting with Beatrice, an envelope arrived for him, directed by her, and enclosing a leaf out of her diary. On this were written, opposite the date of the seventh of September, these significant words :—

" Married, in the Register Office of St. Benedict's, to Stephen Menteith."

She had been right, then, about the date; that is to say, the one in her diary was not the same as that in the Register Book.

But it did not follow, therefore, that hers was correct; the evidence of a young lady's journal would not, Lionel was well aware, be considered highly valuable by an unprejudiced person—it was infinitely more likely for a girl to put down an erroneous date than for a mistake to creep into a public register.

Yet the faintest shadow was worth pursuing, and Lionel determined that he would, at any rate, pay another visit to St. Benedict's, and re-examine the book.

But before starting he sat for some minutes poring over the two bits of paper he had received from Beatrice. He had never possessed any of her handwriting before, and he looked now, with a sort of speculative scrutiny, at the two specimens, which contrasted so strongly with each other, and yet bore the impress of the same character—the delicate, regular, sloping hand of girlhood, and the black, reckless, resolute-looking letters in which the address on the envelope was inscribed. There were the same forms, the same turns; the two were evidently written by one person, yet the difference was striking.

No comment followed the important entry in the diary; apparently it had at this point been brought to a close, for the only other writing on the page, was at the bottom, where these words appeared:

"End of the last journal I shall ever keep."   "Beatrice Clyde."

On the other half of the leaf were one or two entries, but they were dated some weeks before the concluding one; it seemed as if a great gulf had intervened between the time when domestic incidents—girlish criticisms on books, and remarks on picturesque effects of weather—had been noted down, and the day on which that one word of solemn import had been written—"Married"—the word which had changed the whole current of her life, and converted the girl into the woman.

The tenderness of Lionel's pity was as mighty as the passion of his love—he could have wept bitter, manly tears over this last relic of happy girlhood—he yearned as her own mother never had done over the lost hope of a young life—he would have renounced his love, and all desire to see her again, if by so doing he could have blotted out the blight that had fallen on Beatrice, and restored to her the simple, unconscious happiness of fifteen!

But Lionel was not a man to brood long over sentimental fancies—he roused himself, and proceeded at once to the Register Office of St. Benedict's. This time the Registrar was not present, but his clerk came forward, and heard Lionel's request to look at the book. This man, whom Lionel had not seen on his former visit, struck him at once as being like some one he had met, or known, but he could not at the moment remember where, and he was

too intent upon comparing the two dates
to make much effort on the subject.

Something, however, in the clerk's manner of answering the questions—a certain
doggedness and sullen unwillingness to say
anything about the month of September;
185—, fixed Lionel's attention upon him,
and it then occurred to him that this was
the man whom Beatrice had appeared to
recognize, when she had seen him in the
street, at Railton, during the winter assizes.

Certainly he was the same—a square,
stout man, with bullet head, round face,
bead-like, black eyes, and grizzled hair and
whiskers.

The date in the book was as Lionel had
thought — the sixth of September. He
turned the page to see if there was any
entry on the seventh, but none appeared;
and when the next occurred, some days
later, he saw that it did not bear Mr. Cartwright's signature, nor, on turning over
several more leaves, did he again see that

gentleman's name, but another, evidently that of a new Registrar.

"How is this?" he said to the clerk; "I see Mr. Cartwright's signature disappears after the 6th."

"Because he died about that time, I suppose, sir," returned the clerk, taking hold of one side of the book, as if about to close it; "if you have seen what you want, sir, my time is much occupied."

"Do you remember the exact day of Mr. Cartwright's death?" said Lionel, after a moment's thought, and still keeping the book open.

"No—" said the man, rather rudely, "how should I?"

"You were here at the time, though," said Lionel, "for your name frequently appears as a witness. You are called Richard Parker, and I see the name here."

The clerk, who had appeared uneasy for some moments, here turned pale, and said, in a

confused manner, and with marked inci-
vility in his tone:

"Really, I don't see what you have to
do with my name, sir; and you can have
nothing to do with me, and with my signature. Come, sir, we have not time to spend
hours in looking at old entries, and I want
to shut up the book."

Lionel was lost in thought for a minute
—a multitude of ideas rapidly floated
through his brain. This man had been
recognized by Beatrice, yet she had said his
name was not the one she had expected to
hear; he was evidently loth to answer any
questions regarding the period to which
Lionel had referred—he had appeared
uneasy when Lionel had first turned to the
important date—had he any connection
with that entry, beyond that which belonged immediately to his office?

Lionel deliberated within himself whether
he should seek to ascertain what the man
really knew—whether he should try a few

probing questions.   There was some danger
in letting the man know that he suspected
an error in the entry, and that he would
not let the matter rest, since the book was
in the clerk's power, and might be tampered
with, if he had reason to fear the results of
an inquiry; on the other hand, the man
had already been rendered uncomfortable
by the search, and probably placed on his
guard.   Lionel determined, therefore, to
pursue the matter—if the clerk's fears became dangerously excited, he must take
precautions against their effects.

"I know your name," he said, "because
I ascertained it at the Railton Assizes last
winter—you were there as witness in a
nisi prius case; a lady thought she recognized your face, and asked me to inquire
your name."

"And did she recognise that too?" asked
the man, vainly endeavouring to carry off
his embarrassment and anxiety by an appearance of off-hand coolness.

"No," said Lionel, with a searching look, "she expected to hear another—but that is not to the purpose now—what I want to know is the day on which Mr. Cartwright died. I see no signature of his after the 6th; was that the last day that he was able to perform his duties?"

"I don't see what right you have to make these inquiries," said Richard Parker, who became more anxious in demeanour, and more insolent in tone, at every speech; "and unless I know your reasons for asking questions, I shall not answer them."

"Very well," said Lionel; "I have other means of discovering what I wish to know; but, in the meantime, I have business with the Registrar—when is he likely to be at the office?"

"Not at all to-day—there is nothing for him to do, as far as I know, and I am accustomed to transact business for him—could not you tell me yours?"

"My business is with Mr. Bray alone,"

said Lionel; "if he cannot come to me, I must go to him—perhaps you will give me his private address."

The man hesitated, and looked uncertain what to do.

"Stay, you need not," continued Lionel, picking up from a waste-paper box an empty envelope, which had caught his eye before he had asked the question; "this informs me. But it is a long way off—perhaps you will walk with me, and show me the nearest way?"

"I cannot leave the office," said the man.

"Very right," returned Lionel; "and as I do not feel inclined to hunt up the house by myself, and my business will be best transacted here, I shall stay too, and send a message, begging Mr. Bray to come."

And he seated himself at the desk, and wrote a few lines on a stray piece of paper he found.

."And now, will you give me an envelope?—sealing-wax, too," he said, as the clerk, with a sullen air, obeyed him.

"I shall send the note by a cab—will you call one?—you know best where they are to be found."

"I have told you I cannot leave the office," returned Mr. Parker; "and Mr. Bray is not often disturbed in this way—I won't have anything to do with it."

"The man is a poor dissembler," said Lionel to himself; "he thinks I am going to steal or tamper with that book, and I shall certainly not leave him alone with it now."

He walked into the passage, leaving the office door open, and, standing at the street-door, summoned a boy, whom he sent to call a cab. When he returned to the office the clerk was sitting in the place where he had left him, but the Register Book, which was lying on the table, was differently turned. The man had evidently taken a peep at the entry about which it appeared some stir was to be made; but there had not been time for more than a peep.

A cab soon drove up to the door, and the note was despatched. Then the two men sat down together in the office, closely watching each other. Lionel took up a newspaper, but not one of Mr. Parker's movements escaped him. He became more and more convinced that the man had cause to dread any inquiry being made into the circumstances of the marriage dated the 6th of September in the book—more and more inclined to believe that the date in Beatrice's diary was the correct one.

Mr. Bray did not arrive for more than two hours; and Lionel grudged every moment that passed, for he had much to do, if he attempted to ascertain the truth of a suspicion that had occurred to him. He spent the time in reviewing the reasons that had led to his suspicion, and in forming his plan of action.

The two companions never spoke, except when the clerk occasionally gave a hint that it was no use waiting for Mr. Bray—

he was probably too far from home to arrive within office hours; and when Lionel declared his determination to wait, at any rate, till the office was closed.

At length a cab dashed up to the door, and Mr. Bray alighted. He was a nervous, undecided-looking man, with a small, meek voice, and a mild, deprecating expression on his long, thin face. He came in with some flurry of manner, and apologised for his lateness, recognising Lionel as soon as he saw him.

"Ah!" he said, "I thought Constable was the name of the gentleman who visited the office before to look for an entry—I am very sorry that I was out—I seldom take a holiday, but I had gone with my children to an exhibition—really, I am annoyed—so very unforeseen an occurrence—and Mr. Parker is generally able to conduct any business that may arise in my absence—"

"I am sorry for having disturbed you,"

said Lionel; "but my business requires your presence—my time is valuable—I must enter upon it at once."

"To be sure; pray commence, I am quite ready."

"But we are not alone, which I should prefer," said Lionel.

"Oh, I see—Mr. Parker, have the kindness to go into the other office."

The other office, as Lionel knew, was upstairs, and the door at the foot of the stairs was open. Mr. Parker was going to shut it behind him, but Mr. Bray, in obedience to a sign from Lionel, requested him to leave it as it was.

When the man's footsteps had died away on the stairs Lionel spoke:

"I must apologise, Mr. Bray, for seeming to mistrust your clerk; but I have, I fancy, made him suspect that my business relates to him, and it is as well to take precautions."

"I assure you, Mr. Constable, he is a

most trustworthy person," said the Registrar; "he has been in the office longer than I have, and a word has never been said against him."

"He was here in Mr. Cartwright's time," said Lionel, "and I have some cause to believe that the entry I looked at the other day, to which Mr. Cartwright's signature is attached, is wrongly dated."

"But you do not accuse Parker of the error, if there be an error?" said Mr. Bray, rather anxiously.

"I do not accuse him of anything. I have only a faint suspicion that he knows of some mystery connected with that entry —a mystery that I am determined to fathom—and in the meantime, it is important that the book should not be tampered with—you understand."

"Do you mean to imply that my clerk is capable of such a proceeding? I asure you, Mr. Constable, you are making a grave charge—it will be impossible for me to rest easy under the idea—I cannot endure want of confidence, it is exceedingly disagreeable."

"I know it," answered Lionel, "and I am sorry to be obliged to trouble you in this way, but I cannot help begging you to be on your guard; at least to prevent the possibility of the clerk's touching the book without your knowledge."

"But you have told me too little, sir— I would not allow the man to stay in the office an hour longer if I believed he could act in the way you imply—I should not have a moment's peace," said the Registrar, nervously.

"My reasons for suspicion are so slight," returned Lionel, "that they will not justify my saying anything that may injure a man, possibly innocent; and if he has in one instance acted as I suppose, it would be unfair to let that weigh against years of fairness and honesty—I am simply warranted in asking you to take *that* book under your special charge."

"I will do it," said Mr. Bray, "but I must say I feel this is an unaccountable step on your part, and you have made me very uneasy. The responsibility of an office like this is great. I had no reason to mistrust the man, and now I shall be unable to place any confidence in him."

"As soon as I know anything either to restore your confidence, or to give definite form to your doubts, I will let you know," said Lionel. "In the meantime I may tell you, if you can place any trust upon the judgment of a stranger, that I do not believe the man is naturally a rogue. He may once have committed an error, but he has not enough cunning to conceal his fear of being found out."

Mr. Bray clutched at Lionel's opinion with the eagerness of a weak person to be guided by a decided one.

"Then you think I may trust him as before, save in the matter of this one volume?"

"Certainly. It may very likely turn out that my conjectures have no foundation. And I must leave you now. You shall hear from me again in a day or two. Pray forgive me for inconveniencing you so much, and do not, on account of anything I have said, alter your behaviour to Mr. Parker. By the way, did you know anything of the former Registrar, Mr. Cartwright?"

"I did not know him personally—he was a very respectable man, I have heard."

"Yes, I know that. But his disposition, habits, &c., have you ever heard anything of them?"

"I am acquainted with a man who was formerly in his office. I don't know whether you are aware that he was a solicitor? And he described him as a very worthy, well-intentioned person—a little self-important and pompous in manner, as he expressed it, 'a regular cock of the walk,' who would not allow any interference with his claims and responsibilities."

"Thank you. I had an idea that was his character," and, with repeated apologies, Lionel took leave.

He went straight to the Waterloo Station, and started by the next train for Richmond, where the Collingwoods lived.

It was late when he arrived, and something more than dusk when he rang the bell at Mr. Collingwood's gate, recollecting, rather to his shame, that it was the first time he had visited the house since his return to town.

It was a compact little place, suitable for the residence of a comfortable pair like the Collingwoods; and as a neat maid-servant admitted him into the hall, an appetizing smell of dinner greeted his nostrils.

Lionel was rather vexed at having arrived at this hour, for he wanted to speak to Mrs. Collingwood alone, and he imagined that so near dinner-time Mr. Collingwood would not be far from his own fireside.

In fact, as he was announced, Mr. Collingwood rose from his arm-chair, and advanced to meet him with a most hospitable welcome, and a declaration that Mrs. Collingwood, who was dressing for dinner, would be most agreeably surprised to see him.

Mrs. Collingwood entered a few minutes later to speak for herself, and it appeared at once taken for granted that Lionel had come to dinner, perhaps to stay the night; but he prevented any steps being taken for his accommodation by saying that he must return to town by the last train.

"At any rate we shall have your company at dinner," said Mrs. Collingwood. "Mr. Collingwood, will you ring the bell, and order it at once."

Lionel, of course, was happy to stay; but he was rather puzzled as to the manner of introducing the object of his visit.

The dinner was a plentiful, well-arranged meal, and Mr. and Mrs. Collingwood were

too old-fashioned in their hospitality to
allow conversation to be anything but de-
tached, though their voices never rested.

The neat maid-servant waited, and whilst
she was absent for a moment or two,
Mr. Collingwood took occasion to expound
his sentiments regarding male and female
waiters.

"You see," he continued, after she had
returned to the room, "I am a stickler for
old observances, Mr. Constable. Those
Russian dinners, now so much in vogue,
I cannot approve of. I think a host ought
to take pleasure in providing for the comfort
of his guests, and to be proud to carve the
meat for them with his own hands, instead
of entrusting the office to menials. You
will tell me, perhaps, of the 'feast of reason
and the flow of soul,' but, for my part, the
material feast that is seasoned with delicate
attentions, and the flow that is attended
with good fellowship, should always accompany the other—a glass of wine with you,

Mr. Constable?—according to the good old fashion."

"For my part, I like to see what I am going to eat," said Mrs. Collingwood. "The old phrase, 'You see your dinner,' has grown quite meaningless in these days, for no one could mock another so far as to tell him he was expected to dine off glass and confectionary—have a little of this pudding—I can recommend it—that's right. I like to see a young man eat sweets; it's a good sign, as I always tell the young ladies—and I must ask about the young ladies in your part of the world—not that sauce, Mr. Constable?—try the custard—any more marriages? We have often talked over that pretty wedding, have we not, Mr. Collingwood? I assure you, Mr. Constable, those bridesmaids made an impression. There was a wedding in our church the other day — bridesmaids in white hats and blue flowers—very bad taste, I thought, but pretty girls enough

—yet Mr. Collingwood declared that there was not one fit to hold a candle to little Amy Constable, or that handsome Miss Clyde."

" A very fine-looking young woman, that," said Mr. Collingwood. " I am not ashamed of admiring her; and if I were a young man—my dear, I speak freely before Mr. Lionel, for he knew me in my bachelor days."

" And what a gay person you were!" said Lionel. " Mr. Collingwood cannot shock me now, Mrs. Collingwood."

" Ah! you are all alike," said Mrs. Collingwood, with a shake of her head—" gay deceivers all! But I have had no answer to my question—any news of weddings?— anyone looking after little Amy?"

" She has not told her brother," said Lionel; " and poor little Amy is too young a child to dream of lovers."

" Miss Clyde, then?—she is old enough —I mean, I suppose she is past twenty."

" Undoubtedly a young woman of two or three-and-twenty is in the very bloom of her charms," said Mr. Collingwood; "and much more fitted to take upon herself the duties and responsibilities of married life than one of an earlier age. A very young girl thinks more of herself than her husband; and is wanting in that pleasing air of dignity, so becoming in a young matron."

"Miss Clyde is going to be married," said Lionel.

" Indeed!" exclaimed Mrs. Collingwood. "Well, I am sure I am glad to hear of it —she is a person that matrimony will improve and steady. But pray who is the gentleman? — have I seen him? — nay, Mr. Constable, can it be that we are to con——"

"I am not the happy man, I assure you, Mrs. Collingwood," interrupted Lionel; "and you have not seen him. Mr. Menteith only arrived at Wynthorpe just after you had left, and I am sure you did not see him."

"Any previous acquaintance, then?—dear me, the affair seems sudden," said Mrs. Collingwood.

"I do not know any particulars," Lionel said, rather stiffly—"I am only repeating Amy's news."

"But what is he like?—you have seen him, surely—handsome?"

"No, not handsome—an intelligent man —a good talker—rather grave and formal," answered Lionel, compelled to give a description of the man who was only too present to his thoughts.

"I have frequently observed," said Mr. Collingwood, "that very striking, dashing young women marry men of a quiet, studious turn. It is a decree of nature, which generally provides also against two handsome or two ill-favoured people going together."

"There are exceptions to the last rule," said Lionel, politely, to Mrs. Collingwood, anxious to divert the conversation from the subject of Beatrice Clyde.

"Well—I'm sure—we are pretty much as our neighbours, Mr. Collingwood and I— and a woman who has had two husbands has no right to expect two handsome men."

"And the late Mr. Cartwright was a singularly handsome man, from his portrait which I have seen," said Mr. Collingwood, with perfect equanimity.

Here was an opening! Lionel had been wishing all the time to be able to allude to Mr. Cartwright, and feared to do so in the presence of his successor, and the successor himself brought forward the name in the most matter-of-fact manner. The dessert was now on the table, and the damsel had retired, so Lionel scrupled not to take advantage of his opportunity.

"I am afraid you will think my inquiry rather an odd one," said he to Mrs. Collingwood, "but the object of my coming here to-day was to see if you could give me some information about Mr. Cartwright."

" Bless me!—who would have thought of any one wanting information about poor Mr. Cartwright, so long after his death? Well, he was a good man, Mr. Lionel, and I am not afraid of your finding out anything bad about him. Go on—never mind Mr. Collingwood—I assure you he has no idea that I forget my poor Mr. Cartwright, who was a very good husband to me."

" Any inquiry into Mr. Cartwright's merits can only be pleasing to me," said Mr. Collingwood; "and we should always respect the memory of the dead—I can truly say, if through any false delicacy Mrs. Collingwood were to object to speaking of Mr. Cartwright before me, it would be extremely painful to me. It would deprive me of the consolatory notion that, were Mrs. Collingwood to survive me, I should still be mentioned in familiar discourse, and pleasingly remembered when the first grief was over."

"I wish to know, then," said Lionel, seizing upon a pause in the speech, which he feared was not yet finished, "if you, Mrs. Collingwood, can tell me the exact date of Mr. Cartwright's death?"

"To be sure I can—I am not likely to forget it. Ah! it was indeed a memorable day to me—so sudden and unexpected, though poor Mr. Cartwright was not young —indeed we were taken for father and daughter at Brighton—and of a full habit-- yet it was a shock."

"And on what day did it occur?" interrupted Lionel, "it is important to me to know exactly."

"Ah, professionally, I suppose — you lawyers are so mysterious—but I cannot imagine how it can benefit any one to know the exact date of poor Mr. Cartwright's death—however, I can tell you—it was the seventh of September, 185—, early in the morning. He had got up before me, and was dressing, as I thought, in the next room, when I heard a heavy fall—it was apoplexy, and he never spoke again."

"Then he could not have been at the Register Office that morning?"

"Impossible; he had only just got out of bed, poor man."

"And he did not appoint any one to act for him?"

"No, indeed; did I not tell you he was insensible?—and, as far as that went, he never would appoint another person to do anything for him. He had great ideas, as I once told you, of the duties of his office; and even his faithful clerk could never persuade him to stay away on account of illness, or anything else, when he thought himself required."

"Undoubtedly, many irregularities may arise from a contrary mode of proceeding," said Mr. Collingwood.

"Do you know the clerk's name?" asked Lionel.

"I used to do; but I am so stupid at

names. He was a respectable sort of man, and used to come in and have a glass of wine at Christmas. He stayed on as clerk in the office; but of course I have known nothing about the office for years. Barker, or Parker, I think it was. Yes, I have it now — Richard Parker. He was such a round-headed, black-haired man, I used to think."

Mrs. Collingwood pursued the theme of the clerk's appearance for some time, whilst Lionel was considering and combining together the different pieces of information he had gained.

He was so absent that the lady had left the room before he had put to her one or two more questions that had occurred to him. Mr. Collingwood was, however, well informed on the points he wished to ascertain, and told him, without any hesitation, the name of the parish in which Mr. Cartwright had died, and of the church in whose records the register of his death might be found.

" I perceive," said Mr. Collingwood,
" that there is some very important case
connected with these inquiries ; and though
we ought to sacrifice private feeling in the
service of the law, I should, I confess, be
greatly annoyed if anything Mrs. Collingwood has communicated to-day should lead
to her being called upon to produce evidence in public. I am always pained when
I see female delicacy exposed to the scrutiny
of a court of justice. It is subversive, you
know, of all our notions of English reserve,
and if it were necessary for any one to
speak with certainty to dates, I am so perfectly acquainted with——"

" You need apprehend nothing of the
kind, Mr. Collingwood. Neither you nor
Mrs. Collingwood will be subject to any inquiries of a more unpleasant nature than
you have submitted to this evening. I am
the only cross-examiner you need anticipate.
I am sorry to appear mysterious, but——"

" My dear sir—my dear young friend, I

fully appreciate your prudence. Of course
we cannot understand how Mr. Cartwright's
death can possibly bear upon any case in
which you may be engaged; but the
meshes of the law extend far and wide.
But I shall look with interest to the report
of any trial that——"

"I cannot say that there will be any
trial, Mr. Collingwood," said Lionel. "These
investigations of mine may not lead to anything of the kind. I am sorry to have
troubled you and Mrs. Collingwood by re-
ferring to a painful subject——"

"Do not mention it. As I said, Mrs.
Collingwood and I have no reserve on the
point of her former marriage. My dear
Mr. Constable, you are a young man, and
naturally you consider these subjects from
a youthful point of view. Ah! we were all
romantic once! And far be it from me to
deny that romance has its charms. But
when we marry late in life, especially when
we marry a lady who has entered once be-

fore into the married state, we entertain none
of those notions of exclusive regard which
are so fascinating in early youth. I am
aware, of course, that the sentiments Mrs.
Collingwood experiences for me she has
experienced before for another individual.
Shall I, therefore, ignore that that individual has ever existed? No. I assure you
I so highly appreciate the emotion of constancy in the female breast, that I never
discourage the tender remembrance bestowed by Mrs. Collingwood upon her former husband. You know, my dear Mr.
Lionel, we have all had predilections in our
youth. I had not lived to the time of life
I had reached when I married without———.
Well, I will say no more. Can I expect
another person's sentiments to be different
from my own? Though I must say that,
in cases when predilection has not ended in
marriage, I do not think one is bound to
allude to the past. Common decorum and
regard to other persons demand silence.

Therefore, although I am happy to converse with Mrs. Collingwood about the virtues of the late Mr. Cartwright, I do not require her to listen to any experiences of my own romantic days."

" Of course not," said Lionel, who had not been listening.

When they joined Mrs. Collingwood in the drawing-room, Lionel asked her if he might see the portrait of Mr. Cartwright which had been mentioned. She immediately produced it, and it proved to be a photograph—a coloured one, and very well executed, though taken before photography had received the improvements of later years.

" Would you object," said Lionel, " to allowing me to keep this picture for a few days ?"

Mrs. Collingwood appeared surprised, and, for a wonder, did not speak, but looked at her husband.

" I must confess the request is an odd

one," said he ; "and I should be loth to recommend any step which might drag Mrs. Collingwood into public notice——"

"I know it is an odd request," interrupted Lionel ; "but it will not expose Mrs. Collingwood to any inconvenience beyond the loss of the portrait for a few days. Whatever use I make of it will be strictly private. I can promise you that Mrs. Collingwood's name will not be dragged forward."

"If it concerned myself," said Mr. Collingwood, "I should not hesitate. In the cause of justice I would come forward willingly—you need not scruple, Mr. Lionel, to call upon me, if necessary ; but this portrait—it strikes me as suspicious."

"If Mrs. Collingwood has any objection," said Lionel, growing rather impatient of the discussion, "of course I do not say another word. It struck me that the portrait might be useful in establishing a certain——"

"My dear Mr. Constable, take it at once,"

said Mrs. Collingwood. " I assure you I
am not so modest as Mr. Collingwood makes
out ; and nothing could be said of me in
connection with the portrait, even if it were
produced in a public court, except that it
was that of my first husband, and that
I had married again, perhaps, which is
nothing to be ashamed of; so take it, and
welcome. I only hesitated because I was so
puzzled to know what you wanted with it."

" Mrs. Collingwood has decided," said her
husband. " You see, Mr. Constable, we are
not people to throw impediments in your
way ; and whatever cause you are engaged
in must, I am sure, be a just one, and I wish
you every success."

Lionel looked at his watch, and finding
it was nearly time for his train to start,
began taking leave. The Collingwoods were
evidently much excited and bewildered by
his sudden visit and strange inquiries, and,
on the whole, rather pleased at being in
some sort connected with a mysterious

affair. They both accompanied him into
the hall, Mr. Collingwood reiterating his
assurances that he was ready at any moment
to be called upon in furtherance of the
cause of law and justice, and Mrs. Collingwood declaiming on the slyness of lawyers.

" Well, I shall expect to be told some
day," she said—" I understand what pro-
fessional mysteries are—but they must come
out in the end, and then I shall know——"

The rest of the speech vanished in empty
air, for Lionel opened the door for himself,
and disappeared.

He was unable, of course, to prosecute
his investigations on that night; but early
next morning he ascertained by the parish
register that Mrs. Collingwood had informed him rightly as to the date of Mr.
Cartwright's death; and he then proceeded,
with the assistance of those experienced in
such affairs, to find out the particulars
connected with Stephen Menteith's life during the early days of September 185—.

CHAPTER III.

WHEELS WITHIN WHEELS.

BEATRICE CLYDE was just turning away from the village post-office, after despatching her important packet to Lionel, when she saw Stephen Menteith walking towards her. She had chosen to post the letter herself, feeling rather guilty for sending it, and dreading that, if placed in the letter-bag, by some chance the address might be seen.

There was no real harm in what she had done—she was justified in seeking any possible method of freeing herself from the thraldom in which she was held—yet the necessity of concealment was painful to her, and the danger of causing any collision between Stephen and Lionel made her feel timid and hesitating. In spite of herself hope had risen within her heart after her interview with Lionel. He would not, she thought, have attached so much importance to the subject of the dates unless some beneficial result would follow from being able to prove the one in the register to be false.

But her hope was only vague and fluttering—after all Lionel might be mistaken, and the two dates might be alike; and even if different, a mere mistake might not make any important alteration in her position.

The very question, however, of possible escape made her more than ever restless and unsettled; the patience with which she had lately tried to arm herself, and the resigned way in which she had endeavoured to contemplate her future career, as Stephen's wife, had vanished for the present, and his attentions were more distasteful to her than

ever.   She could not help showing some of
the repugnance she felt, and she avoided
private interviews with greater care than
before.

But Stephen was not to be driven back
—he followed her everywhere, seeming as
if he could not trust her out of his sight.
He had watched her after breakfast, and
seen her leave the house; and though then
occupied in conversation with Mr. Clyde, he
had seized the earliest opportunity of following her steps.

He walked rapidly, and was just in time
to see her place her letter in the post-office,
and to meet her as she turned round.

"I should have been happy to walk with
you," he said, "if you had told me you
were going out so early."

"Thank you. I am fond of walking alone."

"It is a habit you will have to give up
at Rio," said Stephen.   "I do not approve
of ladies walking alone, and it is not customary there."

" I suppose I shall do as I am told when the time arrives," said Beatrice.

" I should like you to accustom yourself to consider me devoted to you, and to rely on me for all things before then," said Stephen; "you are so extremely independent, you must always transact all your affairs yourself. If I had known you wished to post a letter you could not send in the letter-bag, I would have done it for you."

" It was no trouble to me to do it myself," returned Beatrice.

" And perhaps you did not wish *anyone* to see the address. Ladies will have secrets sometimes, but I think I might have been trusted."

Stephen tried to veil his real curiosity and suspicion under a lightness of manner which sat unnaturally upon him.

" It was a matter of business," said Beatrice; " hitherto I have not been subject to questioning about my correspondence, and

I think in this one thing I may remain free until I am called by your name."

"I have no desire, I assure you, to be impertinent, or to exercise control over you," said Stephen; "but if the matter is so very unimportant, it cannot signify whether you tell me or not. I do not care for the thing itself, but I should deeply value any proof that you are beginning to have some confidence in me."

"But I have none," said Beatrice, looking up into his face, defiantly; "my opinion of you is formed from the way in which you acted eight years ago, and nothing can alter it. I shall certainly never bestow upon you the most trifling confidence until I am obliged—it would be impossible to guess to what purpose you might employ it."

Stephen ground his white teeth together with vexation. Yet admiration for Beatrice, as she stood with her proud face flushing crimson before him, blazed out of his eyes.

His voice took its softest tone as, after a short silence, he said:

"These are not the sentiments with which married life ought to commence, nor such as I like to hear from you. Beatrice, I would confide everything to you, even circumstances which might seem against me, if I could hope to hear you say our interests were mutual—our love——"

Beatrice interrupted him.

"I have told you before that I can never love you; if you do not wish to disgust me still more, pray leave the subject."

"It is hard upon me," said Stephen, "to be forbidden to speak where I feel so strongly. But it is only for a few days"—and there was a triumphant flash in his eyes —"after we are man and wife in the face of the world, no entreaties shall save you from listening to protestations of my love. You shall know then, if you try to shut your eyes to the fact now, how intensely dear you are to me, in spite of all your defiance and your coldness."

Beatrice half shuddered at his earnestness, but she said, quietly enough :

"True love would prompt very different behaviour from yours ; however, I don't wish to enter upon the question—I only desire to have as much peace as I can during these last days."

Stephen did not attempt to pursue the conversation, and they walked in almost total silence homewards. He did not molest her, either, with much attention for the next few days ; but still she could feel she was ever subject to his watchful scrutiny. Had it not been for the faint glimmer of hope which had arisen within her, she thought the very life must have been crushed out of her beneath the oppression of his suspicious glances, which seemed to follow her everywhere, haunting even her slumbers.

And all the while the weary preparations

went on. Mrs. Clyde and Larkins discussed costumes, and decided what colours became her best—what travelling dress she should wear when she went away as a bride, and whether she should be wrapt in a shawl or burnous. The bridesmaids were invited, and some of them were frequently coming over to assist in settling the important question of wreaths and lappets—the invitations for the breakfast were sent out—the wedding-cake was daily expected—the cards were printed—in short, everything pointed towards that momentous day, the twenty-ninth of November, when Beatrice's sacrifice would be complete; and life, so far as hope and happiness were concerned, would be at an end.

If she was profoundly miserable, Stephen was far from happy. He was uneasy and restless—jealous of any word she spoke to others—ever on the watch to trace some latent purpose in her most trivial action. He appeared to consider her as a fowler

might do a bird not yet completely ensnared;
and every faint, rebellious rising of her
spirit against his seemed to him symptomatic
of a plan to escape.

Beatrice observed that he tried to be near
her whenever she received letters, and that
he scrutinized her countenance as she read
them ; but it was impossible for him to
gather from it any grounds for suspicion,
since no letter arrived which she could not
have read aloud to him.   She scarcely knew
what she had expected ; yet each day, as it
passed away and brought no communication
from Lionel, her heart sank more and more,
and the last spark of hope shone more
faintly.

Only a week now remained of the time
when she would be known to the world as
Beatrice Clyde : a cruel fate, inevitable, in-
exorable, was striding on with giant steps
—each day, long as it was in suffering, was
only too short in reality—each morning
when she woke brought the fearful thought

that one more night was gone, and that thus it would continue, night and morn would succeed each other, until that fatal dawn should rise, beyond which she dared not look, or suffer imagination to picture anything more definite than blank misery —a living death.

It was the afternoon of the twenty-second of November—Mr. Clyde had persuaded Mr. Menteith to ride into Railton with him, and Beatrice, on the plea that the weather looked uncertain, had excused herself from accompanying them. After they had gone, however, the day had brightened a little, and, escaping from her mother and Larkins, she sauntered through the grounds.

The sky was gloomy, but a pale, cold sunshine glimmered occasionally through the branches of the fir-trees beneath which she paced backwards and forwards, between the lodge gates and a side-wall of the little park. The path was retired —cool in sum-

mer, and fragrant with the fresh scent of
the fir-cones—now it was dark and melan-
choly, and seldom frequented, save by
Beatrice, who always sought it when she
could escape from Stephen; partly, perhaps,
because he had never been there with her,
and it was not connected with him by any
association. But she would not be able to
take many walks under the fir-trees now;
this might prove the very last—this day
week she would be far away—where it
signified not—she would be with Stephen
—her husband, whom she hated. Oh! was
there no escape? A wild thought flitted
across her brain—if she were to flee away,
far from all who had ever known her—to
bury herself in some remote spot—happy
only in being free from Stephen! Free!
What madness to dream of Freedom! Even
now a step was behind her, and whose step
was likely to follow her here but Stephen's?

Doubtless he had returned, and was seeking her. Yet, as it drew nearer, the tread

did not sound like his—it was firmer and louder—at once stronger and more buoy-ant. On and on it came, and Beatrice's heart stood still, and then beat loud and wildly, as she turned round, and found both her hands seized and clasped in Lionel Con-stable's.

The sudden rush of joy and surprise died away, and Beatrice withdrew her hands from his, and retreated a step or two.

"Forgive my violence," said Lionel, "my delight overmastered me."

"Delight!" she exclaimed, looking into his face, which did indeed bear marks of a satisfaction which contrasted greatly with the aspect it had worn when they met in Kensington Gardens.

Trembling with hope, sick with suspense, she leaned against a tree, unable to speak further. Lionel, too, was silent for a moment, and stood looking at her with eyes that seemed as if they could never look enough. Then he spoke—

"Your date was the right one—the ceremony took place on the seventh of September, though it was dated as the sixth in the Register."

"Then does it?—oh! can anything free me?" asked Beatrice, in a tone that thrilled through Lionel.

"You shall hear the whole," he answered, exercising strong control over himself, and forcing himself to speak clearly and deliberately. "After I had discovered that the dates were different I examined the book further, and found that Mr. Cartwright's signature no longer occurred in it—in fact, that yours was the last marriage he had registered. I inquired from the clerk the exact date of Mr. Cartwright's death, and something in his manner of refusing to be explicit gave me odd suspicions. I was determined to ascertain all particulars relating to the death, and I was able to do so from Mrs. Collingwood. I need not ask you to follow me through all my inquiries and researches. But listen to this. Mr. Cartwright died on the morning of the 7th of September 185—, quite early. He had never left the house; and yet you, by your own account, were married by him on that day."

"But how? Was my date wrong after all?" interrupted Beatrice, in an agony of dread.

"Stay! Don't alarm yourself," said Lionel, tenderly stretching out his arm towards her for a moment, and then withdrawing it.

With folded arms, standing opposite to her, a few paces off, he continued:

"I wish you would, if you can, give me a full description of the man who married you."

"He was a short, stout, square-looking man," began Beatrice. "He had black hair and whiskers, with a few grey threads in them, a round, rather coarse-looking face——"

. Lionel interrupted her.

"Can you mention any one at all resembling him?"

"Yes," she answered, quickly, "the man I saw in Railton, as we were leaving the Court that day last winter, was so like that I believed him to be the same person, until you inquired the name, and I found it was not Cartwright."

"No; it was Richard Parker, and I am right in my conjectures," said Lionel, with an almost triumphant air, whilst Beatrice hung upon his words with breathless interest.

"Richard Parker is at present a clerk in the same Register Office. He was there in Mr. Cartwright's time, for he told me so the other day, before he had become afraid of my questions, or his behaviour had given me any reason for suspicions. Mr. Cartwright *never* deputed any one to act for him. He died on the day, was dead at the very time, when the ceremony was per-

formed between you and Mr. Menteith.
Your description of the man who did perform it is the description of Richard Parker,
and not of Mr. Cartwright. But stay! —
look at this for a moment," and he paused,
taking from his pocket a small morocco
case, which he opened, displaying within a
coloured photograph of an elderly, white-
haired, florid man, with grey eyes, no
whiskers, a high, bare forehead, well-formed
nose, a slightly pompous expression, and
obstinate-looking mouth. "Does this portrait at all resemble the person who registered your marriage?"

"This! oh no! This is quite a different
person," said Beatrice, in great astonish-
ment.

"Yet this is the portrait of Mr. Cartwright. It was lent to me by Mrs. Collingwood. Then you could positively declare
that it does not represent the man who
married you?"

"Yes, positively."

" And you could swear to the identity of the man who did ? "

" I think so. But would this free me ? "

Beatrice's lips trembled with agitation, and she fastened her eyes on Lionel in an intensity of expectation.

" You have not heard all," replied Lionel. " I have been tracing up Stephen Menteith's actions day by day, during September, 185—, and I find that on the 5th he went to Bristol to make some arrangements about his voyage to South America, and did not return to London till late on the night of the 6th. He and you *could* not have been married on the 6th ; your date, therefore, must be the correct one ; you were married on the 7th, the day on which Mr. Cartwright died. Richard Parker, Mr. Cartwright's clerk, can be identified by you as the man who performed the ceremony. Now, do you see to what all this tends?"

" That the marriage was not a true one?" said Beatrice, breathlessly.

" It could not be a legal one, performed by an unauthorized person," said Lionel; " for some reason, unknown to us, Richard Parker must have consented to personate his master, imitating his signature, and antedating the marriage to avoid future inquiries."

Beatrice clasped her hands together, and uttered a cry of the wildest joy, whilst her whole attitude became expressive of the most intense relief. For a moment or two, there was silence. Lionel and Beatrice stood motionless, some paces apart, but very near in spirit. It was as if a wall had fallen down between · them; and though neither of them dared to give definite form to the thought, they knew that they were really united, heart and soul.

The delicious silence was broken at last. Lionel spoke:

" I ought to tell you that though I firmly believe you have now power to free yourself, it cannot be done without having recourse to legal proceedings; in short, to speak plainly, a declaration of nullity of marriage will have to be obtained from the Divorce Court."

Beatrice grew very pale, even to her lips, but she quickly answered, and in a firm voice,

"It will be terrible, but it must be done. Anything will be better than to remain fettered. At any risk, any sacrifice, I will be free."

"You are right," said Lionel, drawing a step nearer—"the publicity may be painful, but no one can blame you. Some will admire you more than ever—you will believe that"—and he laid his hand on hers.

Beatrice looked in his face for an instant, and read the deep tenderness in his eyes. Her heart was filled with a nameless joy, but this was not the moment to indulge it, nor would he wish her to dwell too much on it. Of that she felt assured—she knew that they understood each other—that there was a confidence between them which no-thing could shake, which needed no looks, no words, no outward signs.

There was a sudden crushing of dead leaves heard; Lionel and Beatrice turned, and saw, advancing towards them, Stephen Menteith. He walked quickly, his face was pale, his lips firmly pressed together. Neither of them shrank at his approach, but stood, with perfect calmness, waiting for him to speak. Beatrice felt just then strong enough for anything; the hope of freedom had penetrated her whole being, and Lionel was with her—her friend, her deliverer.

"I am surprised to see you here, Mr. Constable," said Stephen; "I was not aware of your being in the neighbourhood. It seems you know Miss Clyde's haunts better than I do, for I should not have known where to find her, if the woman at the Lodge had not told me."

"I came with the express purpose of

seeing Miss Clyde," said Lionel, "and I was fortunate enough to observe the flutter of her shawl through the trees."

"The interview has lasted long enough, I hope," said Stephen, with suppressed bitterness; "for it is dusk and chill, and I must beg Miss Clyde to return to the house. When she is gone, I must ask a word or two of explanation from you."

"Whatever there is to explain," said Beatrice quickly, "it concerns me to hear."

"You had better go to the house," said Lionel, in a low tone to her; "I will tell Mr. Menteith all that is necessary."

"I would rather stay," said Beatrice; "perhaps Mr. Menteith will say at once what he wishes to have explained."

"I wish to know why Mr. Constable suddenly appeared here, and why he sought you," said Stephen, growing livid with rage at the cool demeanour of the other two. "I wish to understand why you and he were

so intensely interested in conversation just
now—why his hands were touching yours,
and your eyes were raised to his with
such—" he stopped suddenly, and turned
impatiently from her — then resumed.
"These are questions which it is more fitting
for him to answer than for you, and I would
rather spare you the pain and mortification
of hearing our conversation. Once more,
may I beg you to leave us ? "

"I will not go," said Beatrice firmly ; "I
will remain and tell you myself what you
wish to know. Mr. Constable has sought
me here because he is a true and faithful
friend, and he had news to tell me which
he knew would make me happy. He has
discovered that I am not really bound to
you, and he has come to point out to me
the way to freedom."

Stephen looked in bewilderment from
Beatrice to Lionel, and from Lionel to Beatrice. He tried to speak, but the words
seemed to die away in his throat.

"Miss Clyde has spoken the truth," said Lionel; "she has the means of freedom in her hands—at least, I can give them to her. My interference may appear strange, but I consider her evident desire to escape her thraldom perfectly justifies any efforts I have made to help her."

"Efforts to gain her for yourself, you mean," said Stephen, his voice, ever high-pitched, rising almost into a shriek, with passion. "I know your designs—I know you have been trying to undermine her affections—and no doubt you have now come to her with some plausible story, to make her believe she is not obliged to become my wife. But you are not aware, perhaps, of the actual tie that exists between us?"

"I am aware of the tie by which Miss Clyde believed herself bound," said Lionel— "and I know also that it is really no tie at all;" and he proceeded to relate the circumstances he had already told Beatrice, giving

a clear account of the result of his inquiries.
Stephen listened, too much confounded to
answer. For a few moments a despairing
expression rested upon his face, but it was
replaced presently by a cool, impassive re-
soluteness; and, after a short interval of
silence, he said—

"This is all very fine-sounding, but I
doubt whether, if true, it would free Miss
Clyde. If she declines to consider herself
my wife, and objects to become my wife,
she must prepare herself to appear before
Sir Cresswell Cresswell, a step she is scarcely
inclined to take, I imagine—"

"I am inclined to do anything, rather
than consider myself your wife," said Beatrice vehemently. "I would declare my
history to the whole world rather than
continue to endure what I have endured—
no exposure will frighten me—I will release
myself—"

"This *must* be hatred," said Stephen, in a
low voice, with lips of a deadly whiteness;

"but," he added, in a louder tone, and with an accent of almost savage passion, "though I despair of winning your love, no other man shall enjoy it—I will tear him from you, first—you shall be my wife yet —this day week another ceremony shall unite us, and no one shall have power to part us—whether in love or in hatred, you shall be mine ! "

" I will never—never bind myself to you again !" said Beatrice ; "you must be mad to dream that I will give up the freedom I have gained."

" Will you not ?—we shall see. Remember, unless you are my wife, the contract between your father and me is at an end. If his part is broken, mine shall be broken too. It is still in my power to ruin him, and you through him. Your most ardent friends will scarcely cling to the daughter——"

"Stop !" said Beatrice, hastily ; " we need not drag Mr. Constable into this discussion—it must be between you and me.

But in his hearing I will declare this—that I am ready to brave anything, even to see my father covered with all the shame which your malice can bring upon him, rather than offer a sacrifice which it is a sin to make. I will not, either to save his name or his life, utter vows which I know to be false."

"What does all this mean?" said Lionel to Beatrice, looking with unconscious tenderness at her spirited face; "what power can Mr. Menteith still have over you?"

"He has no power—none, at least, to shake my resolution," said Beatrice; but her voice, now she spoke to Lionel, had lost its firmness, and she seemed weary and exhausted.

"But it must have been from some self-sacrificing spirit that you acted as you did eight years ago?" said Lionel, inquiringly.

"Yes—a mistaken one—but we cannot enter upon it now. I shall never repeat it," said Beatrice.

"I will not hear any rash resolutions," interrupted Stephen. "You must first listen to your father, and consider calmly the fate you will bring upon him, if you refuse to be my wife. This is a question in which Mr. Constable can have no right to interfere, so I should recommend your leaving him, and accompanying me to the house."

The quick, angry blood rose to Lionel's face at Mr. Menteith's covertly insolent tone; but, for Beatrice's sake, he commanded himself, and turned to her as if to know her pleasure.

She spoke firmly, though her hand, which rested on the stem of a tree, trembled visibly.

"Mr. Constable, I hope you will be kind enough to go with me to my father—it is right that he should know everything, and you can explain more clearly than I can."

Lionel bowed, without speaking, and the trio began walking towards the house.

Stephen's face was full of menace, but

he did not attempt to oppose Beatrice's will,
and he forced himself to walk calmly side
by side with the man he hated and the
woman he loved.

It was nearly dark under the fir-trees,
and when they emerged into the open park
the waning light was dim and cheerless.
In perfect silence they walked on, each
heart burning with tumultuous thoughts.
Beatrice was, perhaps, the least excited, for
her resolve was taken, and for the time
being all other ideas were held in subjection
by that master one which had taken posses-
sion of her mind—to remain true to herself,
whatever might ensue.

As they reached the terrace, light streamed
towards them from the house, and as they
entered the hall they were met by Larkins,
who said to Beatrice—

"Oh, Miss Clyde, here you are at last—
your mamma was getting uneasy about you.
She wishes to see you in her room before
you dress."

"Where is papa? Tell mamma I am busy," said Beatrice, hastily.

Larkins looked at her and the two gentlemen in surprise, and then said she believed Mr. Clyde was in his study.

Beatrice signed to her companions to follow, and led the way to her father's private room. She knocked at the door, and then entered.

Mr. Clyde was sitting in an arm-chair, musing by the fire-light; and Lionel, spite of some pre-occupation, for he could not but be aware that there was some reason for considering his intrusion unwarranted, was struck by the alteration in his appearance since he had last seen him. The lines in his face had deepened, a fixed expression of pain contracted his mouth, and there was an air of general languor and helplessness about him which Lionel had never observed in Beatrice's father before.

"Papa, here is Mr. Constable," said Beatrice.

Mr. Clyde looked up in some astonish-
ment, then rose and shook hands in his
usual courtly fashion; but his eyes wandered bewildered from Lionel to Beatrice,
and from Beatrice to Stephen.

The latter was the first to speak.

"Before Mr. Constable says anything, I
wish to have it distinctly understood that I
will not withdraw my claims upon Miss
Clyde. If he succeed in disproving that
she is my wife, I shall still expect her to
become my wife next week; and I shall
look to her father to compel her consent,
otherwise the contract between us is at an
end, and the secret I have had eight years
in my keeping shall be published to the
world.

"Beatrice, what is all this?" asked Mr.
Clyde, trembling, and displeased. "The
contract cannot be broken!—we have fulfilled our part."

"Mr. Constable will explain, papa," said
Beatrice; and she sat down on a low seat

near the fire, throwing off her hat, and leaning her head against the mantelpiece.

"Mr. Constable! What is the matter to him?" said Mr. Clyde. "What business has he to interfere in our private affairs? Excuse me," he added, more mildly, turning to Lionel, "I may appear rude; but I cannot help being surprised at what my daughter tells me—that you have anything to explain—except, indeed, your sudden appearance."

"I do not wonder at your surprise," said Lionel, "and I am conscious that my behaviour must strike you as interfering and impertinent; but I can only beg you to look over it for a moment on account of the important communications I have to make to you——"

He paused for a few seconds, as if to arrange his ideas, and then placing himself on the same side of the fire as Beatrice, and exactly opposite Mr. Clyde, he detailed, as he had done to Beatrice, the result of his

second visit to the Register Office—his discovery of the false date—and the testimony
of Mrs. Collingwood, that her first husband
had died early on the morning of the 7th
of September.

"The 7th was the day when the ceremony was performed," interrupted Mr.
Clyde, half involuntarily. "I can never
forget the date."

"It must have been the day," said Lionel.
"The conviction expressed by you and Miss
Clyde is corroborated by the records of the
ship 'Venture,' which I have sought and
studied. The ship sailed for South America
on that day, taking Stephen Menteith as a
passenger; whilst, from other sources, I
have discovered that on the 5th and 6th he
was at Bristol, making preparations for the
voyage, and did not return to London till
late on the night of the 6th."

"The ship certainly did sail on the 7th,"
said Mr. Clyde, "and Stephen Menteith left
us at the office door to proceed to Bristol,

and go on board immediately. But I cannot see the use of raking up these old things. We are quite satisfied that the 7th was the real date. The mistake in the Register does not affect us now; nor can I conceive of what importance it is to you, Mr. Constable."

"But did you not hear me say that Mr. Cartwright died early on that morning?—that he had never been at the office—and that never in his life had he deputed any one to act for him. But that Mr. Cartwright was not present at the Register Office, though his name appears in the book, the evidence of your own eyes may tell you. This is a portrait of the late Mr. Cartwright, entrusted to me by his widow," and Lionel again produced the photograph.

Mr. Clyde looked at it with interest, and immediately exclaimed, as Beatrice had done, that it bore no resemblance to the person he had supposed to be Mr. Cartwright. Turning then to Stephen, who had been sitting all this time opposite the fire, but slightly withdrawn from the glow it cast around, he said, with some passion—

"Sir, you have been deceiving me. You led me to believe that Mr. Cartwright performed the ceremony. If you knew the truth, you must have been making fools of us. I will have this inquired into thoroughly, and if I find that the marriage was not a true one I will expose you."

"Do not threaten, Mr. Clyde—you might find it awkward to make this matter too public—other things might come to light which you desire to be kept secret. And what interest could I have in arranging a false marriage, and deceiving you? The marriage was for my own advantage—it was my interest to make it binding."

"True," said Mr. Clyde, and he looked again at Lionel, in perplexity. "Let me hear the end of your story, at any rate," he said to him, after a short pause.

"I have not much more to tell," said Lionel; "what I have already said is enough to show that no real marriage took place. It was performed, to a moral certainty, by a man named Richard Parker, a clerk of Mr. Cartwright's, whose identity I have no doubt you and Miss Clyde will be able to swear to. Indeed, she has already recognised him."

"When?—where?" said Stephen, quickly, startled out of his self-possession.

Lionel related the incident which had occurred at the Railton assizes, and his own recognition of Richard Parker at the Register Office; adding,

"The motive for deception on Mr. Menteith's part is indeed incomprehensible; but he may have been deceived himself— the affair rests between him and the clerk. The only reason I have for assuming that he must have known the person acting as Registrar was not Mr. Cartwright, is this— my inquiries about Mr. Menteith's life, eight years ago, have led me to know that he and Richard Parker were upon intimate terms, living near each other, in the district of St. Benedict's. He could not, you see, suppose that the man who acted was Mr. Cartwright, but he might not know that Richard Parker was unauthorised. In any way, the fact is not altered—Miss Clyde is free."

"But she will not long remain so," said Mr. Clyde, looking at Lionel with some haughtiness; "I am still at a loss to understand your interference, and I have no doubt Mr. Menteith will be able to give satisfactory explanations. I cannot help saying to you that I think you have shown bad taste in stirring up this question, when the marriage of my daughter and Mr. Menteith is so near. Whether the first ceremony be valid or not, ought to be of no importance to you."

Mr. Clyde spoke rapidly, to hide an embarrassment which he could not but feel

—he was by no means satisfied that Stephen
Menteith had not deceived him, but he was
glad to catch at any straw to believe him
innocent. He was too much in his power
to dare to indulge any natural indignation.

Lionel coloured, for Mr. Clyde's tone was
wounding to his pride; but he restrained
himself from speaking angry words to
Beatrice's father.

Mr. Clyde saw the effect of his manner,
and he added, half apologetically,

" I did not mean to be rude, Mr. Constable, and I am willing to believe that you
had some better motive for your interference than I can guess; but—there are
circumstances—in short, it is a case in
which we must judge for ourselves, and
nothing that you can say, no doubts you
cast upon Mr. Menteith, can alter the
relations between us. I still consider him
my son-in-law."

" Papa!" exclaimed Beatrice, passionately; " this is a question that I must

decide for myself. If it can be proved that I am not bound to Stephen Menteith, I will have it proved, and I will never submit to become his wife. I am willing to undergo the shame of appearing before the Divorce Court, to free myself. If you will not set on foot the necessary proceedings, you will compel me to place my cause in Mr. Constable's hands."

She blushed violently as she spoke, and then a deadly whiteness came over her, whilst she continued—

"Papa, I am surprised you can still place confidence in Mr. Menteith. He must have known that the tie between us was not binding. Unless it was to please him, could the clerk have cared to deceive us? He has made us feel bound, and known himself to be free. Though the discovery that the marriage was false is the most fortunate thing that could have befallen me, the insult to you and me is not lessened. I

am astonished that it does not alter your
regard for him."

A faint flush rose to Mr. Clyde's worn
cheek, and something like fire darted from
his eyes, as he looked at Stephen. But the
look with which Stephen returned his un-
nerved him, and, leaning back in his chair,
he covered his face with his hands, and
remained for a few moments speechless, from
strangely-mixed emotions.

" Child! child !" he said, presently turning
to Beatrice—" you must have forgotten.
I am in his power, and I must accept him
for what he chooses to represent himself.
True or false, he must be your husband.
You consented once ; and if the marriage
was not a legal one then, we must forget all
about it, and the second——"

" Papa !" interrupted Beatrice, rising and
flinging herself upon the ground at her
father's feet—" there can be no second
ceremony ! I will not do this—I dare not,
even to save you from suffering and shame,

marry a man I hate! I have got an opportunity of freeing myself, and I shall be guilty if I let it pass. I will have all bonds broken between Stephen Menteith and myself—he may do what he will afterwards. Let the worst come, I will stand by you, papa—I will give up everything for you, except truth—I will follow you to the ends of the earth—toil—starve—beg—anything!"

"And you will have friends to help you," said Lionel, advancing a little, and standing by Beatrice. "Mr. Clyde, I am ignorant of the facts of the case — I do not know, nor wish to know, what power Mr. Menteith has over you; but you may be sure that, whatever it may lead to, whatever may befall you, you will not lose your daughter a single real friend—I, for one, will"—he stopped for a second—"I dare not say now what I feel, and it might not be welcome to you; but I dare promise to be her friend till death, if she will allow me."

Mr. Clyde looked helplessly at the animated faces before him; then he glanced towards Stephen, as if to gain from him some idea how to proceed.

Stephen was quivering with rage and mortification; but he commanded his countenance, and said:

"You appear, all of you, to have decided that the marriage was a false one, and with my connivance and knowledge. I will neither confirm nor deny what has been said; but I will make a proposal for Mr. Clyde's consideration. Let Miss Clyde fulfil her engagement and marry me this day week, and I am content to let my character bear the stain Mr. Constable has put upon it, and to abide by the original terms of the contract. But if Miss Clyde declines to marry me—if she attempts to prove in the Divorce Court that the ceremony we went through eight years ago was not a binding one, I will instantly commence proceedings to expose to the world a transaction Mr.

Clyde knows of, but which I will not mention before Mr. Constable, or any one, until Miss Clyde's decision is made. Stay," he added, as Beatrice was about to speak—" I will not receive your answer now. Let the arrangements for the marriage go on—at the end of the week I will hear your decision. I trust common sense and regard for your father will make you more reasonable than you are now; and, meantime, no interference must be used"—and he glanced at Lionel.

"You need not fear me," said Lionel; " I cannot give Miss Clyde any further help, and I shall not offer her counsel."

Beatrice gave him a momentary look, which Stephen saw, and it pierced his heart like a poisoned arrow.

"I think Mr. Menteith's plan is the best," said Mr. Clyde, weakly catching at present relief. "Beatrice will, perhaps, have a little consideration for her father, when she has time to think."

"It is so deceitful!" exclaimed Beatrice. "My mind is quite made up. Why should these preparations go on? I shall never marry Mr. Menteith, let him threaten as he will. He may expose my father—we will bear the shame together, papa. It shall not harm you really. Perhaps," she added, flinging out the suggestion at random, "when all is inquired into, something may be found out which will bring shame upon him as well as upon us. What do we know of his early life? He may have a secret to conceal as well as ourselves."

At these words, weak and womanish as they were, Stephen's face became suffused with a deep red—he started like a person who had been stung, and glanced angrily from Beatrice to Lionel. Then, as if afraid of betraying something, he rose, and walked to the window, looking out upon the dark landscape. None of his movements were lost upon Lionel, but he made no remark.

There was perfect silence, until Stephen again turned towards the group.

"Am I to consider this settled, then?" he said to Mr. Clyde. "I am to receive a decisive answer at the end of a week?"

"I am willing," said Mr. Clyde.

"I have already given my answer," said Beatrice; "but as Mr. Menteith does not choose to take it now, I suppose at the appointed time I shall have to repeat it. If he chooses to have the affair broken off at the very last moment, he can please himself. I am beyond caring what the world may say."

"I trust a week will bring you to reason," said Stephen, quietly, as Beatrice vanished from the room, determined, it seemed, to avoid further argument.

There was another pause, and then Lionel said good evening to Mr. Clyde.

Mr. Clyde looked coldly upon him.

"I still am puzzled at your anxiety to mix yourself up in our affairs, Mr. Constable.

I don't know whether I ought to thank or blame you."

"And I cannot explain," said Lionel; "some day I may be able to do so. If Mr. Menteith fulfils his worst threats, you will then know the reason for my seeming impertinence. You will find in me, though perhaps you consider me officious in now saying so, a firm friend."

"You don't know what you are saying —what you promise," said Mr. Clyde, somewhat touched.

"I don't care what it may be," said Lionel; "shame and disgrace will never keep me from befriending you and—Miss Clyde. Only do not be weak, do not urge her to sacrifice herself — pardon me, I cannot help speaking warmly, and I dare not say anything which might excuse me."

Lionel held out his hand to Mr. Clyde, who took it passively, and let it fall again, as if not knowing whether to be cordial or not.

When Lionel entered the hall, he looked round for Beatrice—he fancied she would not let him depart without a word of leave-taking. He now saw her. She was standing in one of the mullioned windows. He approached her, and said, in a low voice:

"You will be firm?"

"Will I not?" she said, looking up at him.

A lamp was burning in the hall, and by its light he saw her glittering eyes, her flushed cheeks, and fixed determination imprinted on every line of her face. She looked almost fiercely beautiful; but he would not think of her beauty now.

"In spite of threats?" he continued.

"Yes! I will bear everything."

"Could nothing make him relax his stubborn will?" asked Lionel—"nothing induce him to keep your father's secret? What made you throw out that hint just now?"

"Nothing but vain passion," said Beatrice; "but it moved him—did you see?"

"I did. The hit seemed to strike him home. But you know nothing?"

"Nothing of his early life. He did not come to papa till he was a man—there may be something——"

"Enough; if there is anything, I will hunt it out, trust me"—the door of the study creaked on its hinges, and Lionel, with a fervent pressure of Beatrice's hand, left her, and quitted the house.

Mr. Clyde and Stephen were now in the hall, and at the same moment the sound of the dinner-bell reached them—the dressing-bell had rung unheeded half an hour ago.

"Come to dinner at once, Beatrice," said her father, drawing near her. "It will be as well not to disturb your mother with this affair at present."

"I quite agree with you," said Stephen; "let everything go on as before—there is no need for Mrs. Clyde to know anything, until it is finally settled."

"I am indifferent," said Beatrice; "do as you like now—my own mind is made up."

CHAPTER IV.

THE SKELETON OF WYNTHORPE PALACE.

Mrs. Clyde's curiosity as to the reason why her husband and daughter and Mr. Menteith were late for dinner, was appeased by a plausible story, related by the latter, about a prolonged walk under the fir trees, and a chat afterwards in Mr. Clyde's room.

Mr. Clyde and Beatrice said nothing, and a person more observant than Mrs. Clyde would have easily discerned marks of great excitement and disturbance in the manner of both.

"Well," she said, "I am sure it is not tempting weather for late walks, and Beatrice will be getting cold or something, and look wretched next week. But what brought Mr. Constable here? — Larkins saw him in the hall."

"Business, my dear," said Mr. Clyde, roused into paying attention to her words.

"Lawyers are strange beings," added Stephen. "It is their way to make their appearance when they are least expected."

"If he came on business I don't care to hear anything about it," said Mrs. Clyde. "But it would only have been hospitable to invite him to dinner. I dare say, Beatrice, you never thought of it."

"I believe Mr. Constable was on the point of starting for London," said Stephen.

"The business must have been very important to cause such a flying visit," said Mrs. Clyde. "However, as it was business I care nothing about it; only I should think Beatrice might as well have been in her own dressing-room, getting ready for dinner, instead of being present at a law-yer's meeting with her father."

"You forget me," said Stephen, in an assumed playful tone, which grated on Beatrice's ear.

"Oh, I suppose you and Beatrice were entertaining each other. I am sure I don't object to that. I like to see you go on like other people; still you might choose times——"

Stephen interrupted the speech by asking when the two bridesmaids, who were to stay in the house for the wedding, were expected, and Mrs. Clyde's attention was effectually turned into another channel.

The course of outer events remaining undisturbed, she continued in complete ignorance that the preparations, in which she took such deep interest, might never be turned to any purpose at all.

Beatrice was compelled to play her part of bride-elect as before; and if she appeared absent and indifferent, she had appeared absent and indifferent for so long a time, that her behaviour created no surprise.

Both Mr. Clyde and Mr. Menteith were unhappy and unsettled; but any indications of mental discomfort made small impression upon Mrs. Clyde, engrossed as she was with the weighty affairs of trousseau and breakfast. Her ailments were entirely forgotten for the present, and she was never weary. She frequently sent for Amy Constable, who was to be one of the bridesmaids, and who was of incalculable use to her in settling questions of taste, which Beatrice would not consider.

The other bridesmaids were to be Dora and Jessie Lyttelton, Miss Harding, the daughter of a clergyman at Railton, and the two girls already mentioned, who were distantly related to Mrs. Clyde, and were to remain with her some time after the wedding.

In all these arrangements Beatrice had had no voice. It did, indeed, give her a slight, unaccountable pang, to hear that her mother had decided upon inviting Amy

Constable to be one of her bridesmaids; but she maintained throughout an appearance of perfect indifference.

On the afternoon when Janet and Emma Sinclair were expected, Amy Constable was at the Palace; Mrs. Clyde had requested her to go and select her wreath from the six which had just been received from London, before the box was exhibited to the other bridesmaids. Amy, having made her choice, ran downstairs with the wreath on her head, to show herself to Beatrice, who was sitting in the breakfast-room. She found, as she had not expected, Mr Menteith also there —he was standing close by Beatrice, and it was evident to Amy that she had interrupted an important conversation. She was hurriedly retreating, when Beatrice called her to stay, and Amy came forward somewhat confused, thinking Mr. Menteith would consider her absurd with the wreath on her head.

"You look very nice," said Beatrice,

rather absently, as if she felt that something was required of her.

"Mrs. Clyde wished me to have the prettiest," returned Amy; "at least, the most becoming, so I chose this."

"I thought they were all alike."

"Well, so they are to look at in the box, but there are little differences in shape—you see this is rather small across the top, and so it suits me; and there is a lovely little bud that comes just above the ear, don't you see?"

"You are just like mamma, with your minute distinctions," said Beatrice, smiling faintly; "but take off the wreath, and sit down a little, I am sure you have nothing more to do upstairs."

Amy glanced timidly at Mr. Menteith; she did not like him any better than she had done on the night when she had driven from Railton with him and Beatrice, and she felt that her presence was quite as unwelcome to him now as it had been then. But she saw that Beatrice wished her to stay, so she sacrificed herself on the altar of friendship, and, taking off the wreath, sat down by the fire.

"I must not stay much longer, though," she said; "for it is very damp and raw this afternoon, and mamma will not like me to be out late; but Mrs. Clyde says she wishes me to stay and see the Miss Sinclairs—I suppose she wants us to be friendly, as we shall see a good deal of each other when you are gone."

"Perhaps," said Beatrice; "and you are such a favourite with mamma, that she cannot do anything without you."

"I am sure we ought to congratulate ourselves that Mrs. Clyde has met with a young lady like Miss Constable, to supply your place, to some extent, Beatrice," said Mr. Menteith, with strong emphasis on the *we*.

He delighted in speaking as if he and Beatrice were already one, in the presence of the uninitiated, when she was unable to contradict him.

Beatrice bit her lips, but said nothing; and Amy glanced from one to the other, half afraid of them, and confirmed in her notion that they were the oddest pair of lovers she had ever encountered.

By way of diminishing the awkwardness that was growing round the whole party, she began to talk, but no subject presented itself to her mind that was not, in some way, connected with the approaching marriage.

Stephen encouraged her to proceed—it gave him a sort of satisfaction to hear the wedding spoken of as a fixed, irrevocable thing. He, however, was far from feeling confident himself—neither eloquent pleading nor terrible threatening had induced Beatrice to waver from her purpose; she cared not for his love, and she defied his power.

So she sat, pale and scornful, but with her heart bleeding inwardly at the thought of the misery and disgrace she was going to bring upon her father, whilst the other two conversed.

A noise in the hall aroused the attention of all three; and suddenly, without announcement, Mr. Carleton, in hunting costume, walked into the room.

Beatrice hailed his appearance as a relief; she knew that Amy, in his presence, could not continue the theme that had engaged her, and she was, besides, always glad to see Mr. Carleton, who had, she well knew, ever been her advocate, and who was, too, a friend of Lionel Constable's. She felt also, instinctively, that he understood her, and believed her engagement with Stephen to be repugnant to her; so her manner was warmer than usual, as she welcomed him, and listened to his account of the chance that had brought him.

He had lost the hounds, and, finding himself near the Palace, had called for a few minutes' chat by the fire, before turning homewards. Mr. Carleton could not help being struck with .the appearance of Beatrice; the agitation of the last few weeks had left its marks upon her, and though her beauty was not of a kind to depend upon complexion or good spirits, there was a care-worn, haggard look about her face, which would have made a stranger imagine her several years older than she was.

The air of constraint, too, that was apparent between her and her betrothed did not escape Mr. Carleton's observation, and he wondered, as he had done many times before, what strange fate had brought two such incongruous beings together. After some trifling remarks had passed, Mr. Carleton said,

"What has become of Lionel, Miss Constable? He was in Railton the other day, and never came near us."

"In Railton!" exclaimed Amy, in great surprise; "he has never been at home since he left us so suddenly in September."

"He was in Railton, at any rate," returned Mr. Carleton; "he must have been about some very pressing business not to be able to peep in upon you; however, I no longer feel aggrieved, as he did not even find time to visit you."

"But how do you know he was there, if you did not see him?" asked Amy.

"I heard he had been in the town from Headly, of the Grammar School, who told me he had been at his house last Tuesday night, inquiring the address of that Mr. Desmond who lectured, you know, at the Institute, and called you young ladies darlings. What he wants with the famous Brian Hope I know not—I trust he is not going to draw the poor Irishman into a lawsuit. However, it is a great chance if he finds him, for he is likely enough to be at the Antipodes by this time, or as far on the way as it is in the power of steam to take him."

During this speech Stephen Menteith

changed his attitude uneasily once or twice, and at last, taking a newspaper from the table, almost screened his face with it.

Beatrice looked at him searchingly, and a quick flush rose to her face; she did not speak, and it was not necessary, for Amy poured forth a torrent of questions to Mr. Carleton about Lionel's movements.

"I know nothing," he answered, "beyond what I have told you—I expected news from you, and you ask it of me."

"It is very odd!—Lionel never told us he was coming to Railton," said Amy; "he wrote a week ago, and never mentioned anything about it."

"I suppose he did not know he was coming, a week ago—the business that brought him was sudden, most likely," said Mr. Carleton, and he began to talk of something else.

Mr. Menteith had by this time recovered his self-possession, and the conversation was almost entirely supported by the two gentlemen till Mr. Carleton rose to go.

He looked at Beatrice with real pain as he said good-bye—he was so thoroughly impressed with the conviction that she was unhappy; and meeting Mr. Clyde in the hall, and observing his hollow eyes and uncertain manner, he arrived at the conclusion that the father, as well as the daughter, was ill at ease on the near approach of the marriage.

"There is some secret misery under all the gay show," he said to himself as he rode away; "the skeleton supposed to be hidden in every house certainly lurks in some corner of Wynthorpe Palace. I would do anything to save that girl from her fate —the man is not worthy of her, and she will be utterly sacrificed."

Amy took advantage of Mr. Carleton's departure to make her escape to Mrs. Clyde's dressing-room; she really felt incapable of submitting any longer to the *gêne* of assisting at an interview between the betrothed pair.

Beatrice and Stephen were left together once more, but they did not talk much. Beatrice was silent, because she wished to pursue a train of thought stirred by the few words spoken by Mr. Carleton about Lionel Constable; and Stephen's thoughts followed the same direction.

He began to feel strong misgivings that Beatrice would escape him—nay, perhaps, he might also miss his revenge—he might lose Beatrice, and fail to embitter her future life. Yet the mere sight of her seemed to give him some hold over her; and whenever she made an attempt to leave him, he contrived to detain her by some question, to which she was forced to give an answer. He had not made a single effort to deny or disprove the story, Lionel Constable had related, about the irregularity of the ceremony that had made Beatrice believe herself his wife. In fact, Lionel had ascertained so fully the course of his actions during the critical days in question, and was so well provided with evidence to support the truth of his assertions, that Stephen judged it best to preserve silence about the matter, and to confine his energies to the business of obtaining Beatrice's consent to marry him at the appointed time.

He did not try to make her love him—that, he was assured, was a hopeless task—he must work upon her by terror now, and afterwards, when she had fairly become his wife, use all his tact and talent to gain her heart by degrees.

He little understood Beatrice, or the strength of the spirit that supported her; and he calculated upon her fear of the remarks of the world, if she broke off her engagement at the last moment, and yet more upon her affection for her father.

As the sounds of carriage-wheels announced the approach of the Miss Sinclairs, he turned to Beatrice and said—

" I hope you will be on your guard, and not betray to your friends your dislike for me."

"I do not care what they think," she answered; "in a few days they will know the truth."

" You do not know what you are saying," said Stephen; " I can never believe that when matters are so far advanced you will have courage to draw back."

" I would draw back at the very altar," replied Beatrice; and she left the room to meet ner guests in the hall.

She passed the evening in painful attempts to appear interested in the girlish talk of the Sinclairs, whom she had not met for several years. They were rather puzzled by her behaviour, and thought her different from the Beatrice they remembered; though, as Janet said to Emma, when they were going to bed, " Beatrice never had seemed like other girls."

" And Mr. Menteith ! " said Emma; " I

am not sure that I like him much—he never takes his eyes off Beatrice, and I heard him speak very strangely to her once or twice."

" She snubs him rather, I think," said Janet. "I know if I were a man going to be married, I should expect different treatment. Altogether, it is an odd household. Mr. Clyde looks dismal, and starts up every now and then to be polite ; and Mrs. Clyde is for ever fidgeting about Beatrice's things."

" Ah ! I daresay that annoys Beatrice, and makes her seem so indifferent at times. Well, there is to be a grand dance after the wedding, so we shall get that fun out of it. It always is best when the bride and bridegroom are gone."

The next day was Sunday—a long, weary day, without the distraction of worldly business to prevent Mrs. Clyde and the Sinclairs from observing the conduct of the three members of the circle who were oppressed by a burdensome secret.

Mr. Clyde was more miserable than ever, wondering in what position another Sunday might find him ; and he could not rest without summoning Beatrice to a private interview after church, and trying to work upon her feelings, by drawing a vivid picture of the shame and wretchedness she would bring upon him, if she persisted in her refusal to marry Stephen.

But Beatrice was immoveable; her heart was wrung with anguish—she bore all the pain of feeling that she was blamed as unnatural and selfish; and only replied, at the close of all her father's entreaties—all appeals to her filial duty :

"I know it all, papa; I know what will happen, and I am wretched; but I cannot sacrifice myself again—I dare not, even to save you!"

So the interview ended in disappointment on the one hand, and renewed grief on the other.

Beatrice went to church again in the

afternoon, though her mother told her that it was not etiquette to go even once the Sunday before her marriage; and, of course, Stephen went also.

As they were leaving the church, he whispered to her:

"Next time we leave this place we shall be *one !*"

Beatrice shuddered, and shook her head.

She tried to overtake the Sinclairs, who were a little in advance; but they had been joined by Amy—and Stephen, muttering, "I am not going to walk home in a crowd," resolutely drew her arm within his, and she was compelled either to remain with him, or to make her resistance conspicuous in the sight of her neighbours, which she did not care to do. She could defy the world in great matters; but, in a trifling affair like the present, the result was not worth the effort.

The girls took care not to loiter so as to interfere with the betrothed; and Stephen and Beatrice walked together along the road, like lovers. As soon, however, as they were free from all observation, Beatrice withdrew her arm, and accused Stephen of being anxious to parade their supposed position in the eyes of all who knew them.

" I own it," said Stephen; " I am proud of you, and I wish every one to know that you are going to be my wife."

" You know all the time that I will not be your wife !" returned Beatrice.

" I cannot believe your resolution will hold out," said Stephen, professing a faith he scarcely felt. " You will shrink from facing a Divorce Court, and you will not condemn your father to the misery that awaits him if I expose his guilt?"

" I will bear anything — it is no use speaking to me," said Beatrice, setting her lips firmly together.

" You will not like your friends to see a case in the *Times* headed ' Menteith *versus*

Menteith,' pursued Stephen ; " you will not like the men who have dangled after you to become aware that all the while you encouraged them you believed yourself to be a married woman. Few of them will be ready to stand by you then, or to renew the flirtations which my arrival interrupted. Even your warmest champion will think twice before connecting himself——"

"I will not bear this!" exclaimed Beatrice, vehemently, her flashing eyes and glowing cheeks showing how much his words roused her. "I know all the consequences you predict, and I care not for them. But it is needlessly insolent to remind me of them—a *gentleman* would not have done so. And I am surprised at you, for hitherto you have generally acted your part marvellously."

Stephen turned pale, and the working of his mouth betrayed his wounded vanity.

He was silent for a short time, and when he again spoke he tried a different tone.

"You should allow something," he said, "to my great anxiety. If I employ unjustifiable arguments, you should set them to the account of my great love. Beatrice, I do love you, deeply and passionately. Consent to be mine, and I will devote my whole life to make you happy. I cannot—no, I *will* not bear to lose you. You *must* be my wife," and he fastened his eyes upon her with an expression of such despairing fondness, that Beatrice's compassion was, for a moment, touched. It was awful to be loved in this manner by a man she could not even respect. She did not believe that his love was pure and noble, like Lionel's; but still it was love—strong and persistent —and it could not be turned from and forgotten as a thing of no moment.

Yet she did not relax for one instant her strict determination never to yield an iota to Stephen's prayers, or to his threats; and she again declared her firm resolve to break off the match and bear his vengeance.

They were just then passing a small clump of trees that skirted the footpath, and suddenly a man appeared from the midst of the thicket, walking straight towards them, as if to attract their attention.

The moment Beatrice saw his face she recognized him, even by the dim light, as the man she had seen at the Railton assizes, and once before in her life; but whose name she had not known to be Richard Parker.

Stephen and he stared at each other; and just as Richard Parker seemed about to speak, Mr. Menteith made a sign of silence, and said to Beatrice—

"May I ask you to walk on alone, Miss Clyde? This person has, I believe, some business with me."

"Whatever business he has with you must concern me," said Beatrice, "and I should be foolish to leave you together to plot against me."

Stephen slightly smiled.

" Yes, I understand," she continued.
" Of course you can meet without my
knowledge. I am no match for two cunning men ; but still I will not give you this
chance. I will hear what this man—who
has been your tool, or your accomplice—
has to say—why you have summoned him."

" Do not be unreasonable, Beatrice. I
have not summoned him. I am as ignorant
as yourself as to what has brought him.
But I can hear what he has to say another
time. Allow me, at present, to escort you
home."

" I cannot wait your pleasure," said
Richard Parker, breaking silence, and
speaking with much hurry and confusion ;
" and it is all the same to me whether the
lady hears me or not. It seems to me that
I am a ruined man, *Mr. Menteith* ; and as
you are clever enough to ruin or to raise, I
am come to you for help how to get out of
the scrape. I travelled last night from
London on purpose to see you, and I must

go back to-night—to my work to-morrow—
if I go back at all, so I have no time to
lose."

"You have chosen an unsuitable time
and place for an interview," said Stephen.
"Why did you not go to the house, and
ask to see me privately?"

"I have been there; but you were at
luncheon, and occupied, they said; so I
got no admission. I watched you to church
this afternoon, and waited for you here. I
suppose if I were to go to the house again
I should be told you were at dinner, and
so my journey would end in nothing. And
what I have to say is this—a gentleman has
been poking into that Register Book you
know of."

"We know all that," said Stephen; "if
that is all your business, you may as well
take leave."

"That's the way you turn over an old
friend in distress, Mr. Menteith," said Richard Parker, taking a half-menacing tone;

"it may be as bad for you as me in the end,
perhaps, and you'd better make common
cause with me, instead of leaving me to
shift for myself. I tell you the matter is
not going to rest here—that fellow, who is
a lawyer, and a sharp one, too, has some
reasons of his own for sifting this affair, and
he has taken care to be beforehand with me
—in one way, at any rate. Of course, when
I thought that entry was going to be brought
up against me, and you too, as far as that
goes, I was not going to be so foolfsh as to
let it stand a witness against me in the
book—you understand—but when I looked
for the book after the lawyer had had a
meeting with Mr. Bray, which you may be
sure I tried to prevent, I could not find it
anywhere ; and Mr. Bray—a softish sort of
man, generally, was as dumb as an oyster—
I could not get anything out of him, except
that, for business purposes, the book had
been removed. And he has never even
hinted the shadow of an accusation against

me, and we have gone on as usual ever since. Still, it is impossible for me to be easy with this hanging over me; and you would have seen me last Sunday, for I had made out at the warehouses where you were, only I then had hopes of making something out about the book."

"My good fellow," said Stephen, speaking more cordially than he had done before, "so far as I can see, you have no cause to trouble yourself or me about the matter. For my part, I am glad you were prevented playing any tricks with the book—it would have been shallow knavery, which never answers. You would have been suspected at once. Now, if you only keep yourself quiet, no harm may befall you."

"I tell you," said the man, earnestly, "the affair is not finished—they are only throwing dust in my eyes, and as sure as you and I stand here, we shall be called upon to answer in a court of justice for the transaction of that morning."

"I don't apprehend any such unpleasant consequences," said Stephen, composedly; "who do you suppose has any interest in proving anything against that marriage?—what good would be gained by it? Look you, this lady is to be married—married in that church—to me, on Tuesday; after that, who will care to bring up old stories that might tell against you?"

The man looked from Stephen to Beatrice, and the gesture of denial and indignant exclamation made by the latter did not escape him.

"That may, or may not be," he said; "there's many a slip betwixt the cup and the lip; and my safest plan, I take it, since you can give me no better advice, is to bolt at once—only, Mr. Menteith, I must have the means—if I lose my situation, you owe me something."

"If you take my advice, you will not lose your situation; but I refuse no moderate compensation for any alarm you have suffered," said Stephen, blandly; "as to running away, it is a foolish scheme, and compromises you directly, and irrevocably."

"But as long as I am safe out of the law's clutches, I don't care."

"But how do you know when you are safe? If matters were to proceed to the extremities you fear—which they will not, shall not—you might be caught, and you would stand in a thousand times worse position than if you had stayed, fulfilling the duties of your situation. I tell you, man, there is no cause for fear."

The apparent confidence of Stephen seemed to impress Parker.

"If I could keep my place, and nothing was said about it, I should be foolish to cut," he said, doubtfully; "but I don't know that you are altogether a fair judge; and you may only say these things to let all the blame fall on me, whilst you get through scot-free yourself."

"I assure you I have no intention of

absconding, and being missed on the bridal morning," said Stephen; "after that you need fear nothing."

"Even before Tuesday something may happen," objected the man; "and the lady does not seem of the same mind with you about the said wedding. No—I had better be off—you have done me no good—but that compensation you speak of must be forthcoming."

"I will give you nothing unless you promise to go back to your situation, and keep quiet for two days; if you do that, you shall receive with my wedding-cards this——" Stephen took out his pocket-book, and wrote some figures on one of the leaves. "You have never known me break a promise yet, have you?"

"As to money-matters, you have always been a gentleman, St—— Mr. Menteith; but how if there is no wedding?"

"In that case the sum will still be yours, and you will have my permission to go where you will. If any change occurs, if any danger threatens"—he lowered his voice to a whisper—"if it is no use to keep up appearances any longer, I will give you warning—I know we are discovered; but my marriage will prevent further steps being taken, and you will thank me for saving your place and character."

" To say nothing of stopping ugly suspicions against yourself—well, I trust you till Tuesday; but if you are not married on that day, you must not fail to send me a telegram."

"I promise," said Stephen ; " but the marriage will take place, and you may make your mind easy."

"I would not be too sure if the lawyer and the lady are in league," said Richard Parker, in a low tone; and, with a shuffling bow to Beatrice, and a nod to Stephen, he moved away, and walked down the road towards the village.

Beatrice and Stephen proceeded homewards in silence. The latter was not sorry that Beatrice had witnessed the interview between him and Richard Parker. He knew that it was no use trying to make her believe that no fraud had been practised against her with regard to the register marriage—so the man's admissions which she had heard did not give him any concern; whilst he thought, on the other hand, that the confidence he had himself expressed might produce more effect upon her ; also, the idea that the man, whom it was so important for her to iden-tify as the person who had performed the marriage ceremony, might escape, would fill her with alarm. He said to her, just before they reached the house :

"You insisted upon hearing the conver-sation that has just passed; it must have shown you, I think, that your friend, Mr. Constable, has reckoned too confidently upon his power of proving that ceremony to have been performed by an unauthorized person."

" I don't know how far this man's absence might injure my cause, in a legal point of view," said Beatrice, with outward firmness, though she was inwardly trembling as to what might be the consequences of the threatened flight of Richard Parker; " but I know this—that the ceremony that took place binds me to nothing; and that nothing shall induce me to take part in one that would really bind me to you. There may be some doubt about my position in the eyes of the world; but I shall be free to the satisfaction of my own mind and my own conscience. I have now been face to face with the person who was passed off as the Registrar; I know what he really was, and I am ready to swear at any moment that he was the man who performed the ceremony."

" Yet it will be little use if he is not forthcoming," said Stephen.

" I tell you, I am satisfied with knowing that I am free; " said Beatrice passionately, for Stephen's tone irritated her.

"You must see," continued Stephen, after looking at her intently, as if to read her most secret purposes, and yet with involuntary admiration at her spirited glance; "you must see that I have no fear of losing you, or that your champion" —with a sneer—"can really separate you from me, or I should have seized at the idea of Richard Parker's flight, and approved instead of blaming his intention of tampering with the register."

"Your conduct in this proves nothing," returned Beatrice; "you said yourself that shallow knavery did not answer, and I for my part have always given you credit for too much cleverness to form or carry out a bungling scheme. Besides, for all I know, you may wish to keep some evidence that there was a ceremony performed, though there is a chance of its being proved to be false. Oh, I assure you, 'shallow knavery' is the last thing of which I suspect you."

There was a bitter emphasis on the last words which stung Stephen to the quick; he looked into her face—for they were just passing into the lamp-light of the hall—hoping to trace some mark of weakness which might belie her words—but she stood calm, pale, and proud before him. Strange that her scorn and aversion seemed only to increase the overpowering passion he experienced for her! He said nothing; but, giving her one of the candlesticks from the hall table, gently pressed her hand—a liberty upon which he rarely ventured, so determined, he declared himself, not to receive the slightest favour unwillingly bestowed, until she was irrevocably his—and darted towards her a look of love, which revolted her more than his most menacing glance.

Proud and calm as she appeared, she had no sooner reached her own room than a burst of indignant tears relieved her heart—relieved, at least, the passionate wrath that his words and looks had kindled. The incident of this afternoon filled her with a thousand new fears. After all, it might be impossible to establish her freedom— there might be a fearful ordeal to undergo, and yet no certainty of complete relief. She might allow her name to be dragged before the public—she might condemn her father to ruin and disgrace—and yet she might not, in the sight of the world, be entirely released from the tie between herself and Stephen Menteith.

But she did not waver. She would dare everything,—blame, misconstruction, misery and shame to others, pain and grief to herself, for the mere chance of freedom. Nay, as she had said to Stephen, nothing could now deprive her of the precious feeling, that, before her own mind, and her own conscience, whatever the world might say or doubt, she was free!

CHAPTER V.

THE HONOUR OF BRIAN HOPE DESMOND, ESQ.

EARLY on the morning of the day after his visit to Wynthorpe Palace, Lionel Constable found himself on the platform of the railway station at Bangor. He had travelled all night, and was now near his destination —the abode of Mr. Desmond—at least if the address Mr. Headly had given him should prove correct, which very possibly might not be the case, so uncertain were Mr. Desmond's movements, so wandering was his disposition. He was supposed at present to be engrossed by a project for making picture-frames of slate, and to have

L 2

established himself for the purpose of carrying out his ideas on the subject in the neighbourhood of the Penryhn slate quarries. Mr. Headly did not know the name of the place where Mr. Desmond had pitched his tent, but Lionel, after making inquiries at the station, decided that in all probability he would be found at a little town formerly named Bethesda, and now also known as Llan Ogwen, which was chiefly inhabited by persons employed in the quarries.

He engaged a car at the station, but various delays took place, and it was nine o'clock before he was on his way to Bethesda. It was a chilly, drizzling morning, and a veil of thick mist hung over Penmaen Mawr and the sea, whilst the hills beyond the quarries stood out dark and threatening against the cold grey sky. Lionel was too intent upon his search to notice the face of the country through which he passed; all he cared for was speed, and even the careless, rattling pace of the Welsh driver up and down hill was not quick enough for him. Past the leafless woods of Penryhn, the model cottages of Llandegai, above the deep romantic gorge, romantic haunt in summer days, but now dim and dreary, shrouded in November mist, across the bridge over the swollen Ogwen stream, Lionel was hurried on, heedless of anything save the now distinct growing outlines of a bare-looking little town, standing in the shadow of the dark hills. Arrived at Bethesda, slate-built capital of a slate world, Lionel drove up to the door of the inn, and inquired whether Mr. Desmond was known in the town. He soon made out that a person of his description—the name of Desmond did not appear to have made much impression upon Welsh ears—was lodging in a house on the side of the town nearest the quarries, and thither accordingly he directed his steps. The woman of the house spoke English, though not of very

intelligible sort, and she informed Lionel
that her lodger had gone out, she believed,
to the quarries ; but that, if the gentleman
would walk in, she would send her little boy
in search of him.

Lionel, therefore, was ushered into an
apartment, which he concluded to be the
sitting-room of Mr. Desmond. There was
a small fire in the grate; and the window
was partly open, probably in order to re-
move the odour of stale tobacco, which was
still sufficiently perceptible. A strange
medley of articles, which evidently did not
belong to the owners of a Welsh lodging-
house, littered the room ; some water-colour
sketches, of considerable power, were spread
on the tables ; books of all sorts were scat-
tered about; a large engineering map was
half-uncoiled on the floor; a copy of Horace
lay open upon a small round stand, on which
an empty cup and saucer and a plate of dry
toast yet remained—relics of Mr. Desmond's
breakfast ; whilst on the mantel-piece, vari-

ous rolls of paper were huddled together—
some partially open, displaying designs for
picture-frames, cornices, &c. Some slabs of
slate were propped against the wall, and
chips of the same material strewn about,
made the floor of the room rather uncomfortable walking for people who were lightly
shod. A box of water-colours was open in
the window-seat, and an unfinished drawing
hung on an easel, near which brushes,
colour-tubes, and palettes seemed to have
been flung about in dire confusion.

Lionel had plenty of time to become
acquainted with all the articles in the room,
and to know by heart the features of Thomas,
Earl of Courtland—an engraving of whom
was suspended over the chimney-piece by a
bit of string; and which, according to the
inscription it bore, had been presented " to
his esteemed friend, Brian Hope Desmond,
Esq."

He began to grow terribly impatient for
the return of the landlady's son; and at

length, determined not to lose more time, he announced his intention of proceeding to the quarries himself, directing the land-lady to tell Mr. Desmond where he was, in case he should return first.

The rain had ceased, and the sun was faintly struggling through the clouds, when Lionel entered the vast area formed by the slate-quarries. As he looked and beheld the numerous terraces, where the slate was being worked by invisible means—not a creature being distinguishable to his unaccustomed eyes—it appeared to him almost hopeless to seek for an individual man in this stupendous scene, where nature seemed so great, hu-manity so small.

He quickly collected his energies, however, and addressed himself to the pursuit. He was soon accosted by a man, who inquired whether he wished to be shown over the works. He replied in the negative, but asked if Mr. Desmond was known there, and where he was likely to be found.

The man smiled, and answered directly:

"Oh! the Irish gentleman who comes every day to split slate? I saw him not ten minutes ago; if you'll follow me, sir, I can point him out to you."

Lionel followed his guide, and was led presently to a small shed, where Mr. Desmond, in company with two or three quarrymen, was busily engaged in cleaving slabs of slate. He was intent upon his work; but Lionel's shadow coming between him and the light made him look up.

"Oh! by my faith!—and is it you, Mr. Constable?"

"I am glad you have not forgotten me, Mr. Desmond," said Lionel; "for I have come to beg a favour of you."

"Forgotten, indeed! I'm not the man to forget my friends. No; I never forget the face I have once seen, the name I have ever heard, or the voice I have listened to. But what chance has brought ye here?—ye find me in the midst of my labours; manual-work—the finest thing in the world to regenerate humanity, or to create an appetite. Just try your hand a bit at this cleavage — ye're a gentleman, sir, and a scholar, and I'll back ye against any of these mere mechanical labourers."

"But, sir," began one of the men, "you haven't split a single slate yet, according to your intentions."

"Nonsense, man—mere accidents; and my system is not matured yet; when it is, I'll show ye——"

"But, Mr. Desmond," interrupted Lionel, rather impatiently, "my business with you is important. May I ask you to leave your work for a short time, and walk with me towards your lodgings?"

"With all the pleasure in life," said Mr. Desmond;" and he put on his coat, preparatory to starting; but still a considerable time elapsed before Lionel could tear him from the spot. And afterwards he wished to commence a tour round the quarries, saying they could talk by the way. Lionel resisted all persuasions, exhibiting a lamentable want of an inquiring spirit; and succeeded at last in inducing him to take the road to Bethesda. There was something in the earnestness of Lionel's tone which commanded attention; and Mr. Desmond now listened to him more patiently than might have been expected. Lionel began telling him that Miss Clyde and Mr. Menteith were upon the point of marriage; that Miss Clyde was desirous of breaking off the match, into which she had been forced by circumstances; but that Mr. Menteith kept a hold upon her, by means of his acquaintance with a secret affecting her father's prosperity and good name; which secret he threatened to disclose unless the engagement was fulfilled.

"Now, Mr. Desmond," continued Lionel, "you once hinted that you knew some particulars of Mr. Menteith's early life, which he did not wish to have published to the world. It is true that he denied all knowledge of you, but that only supports the notion that he had some reason to fear you. At all events, putting together all I remember of his behaviour and yours, during your visit at Railton, I cannot help drawing the conclusion that you may give some information about Mr. Menteith's former career, which may enable Miss Clyde to place him in check, and stop his threats with respect to Mr. Clyde."

" Ye mean, that if ye'd a secret to hold over his head, he would keep Mr. Clyde's secret ? "

" Just so," said Lionel.

" And ye think to get that secret out of me ? No, no, Mr. Constable, the honour of the Desmonds forbids that. If I do know anything to the discredit of Mr. Menteith, it is sacred with me—all the more because he suspected me," said Mr. Desmond.

" I should be sorry," said Lionel, " to ask

you to do anything against your honour; but this is a case in which, it appears to me, ordinary considerations should give way. Miss Clyde is most painfully situated—either she must marry a man she dislikes, or be the means of bringing terrible misfortune upon her father."

"I feel as much for Miss Clyde as a man can do," said Mr. Desmond; "she is far too good and beautiful to be 'thrown away upon a sneak like Menteith; besides, when was Brian Hope Desmond insensible to an appeal for a woman in distress? Bless the sex! he loves them all too well to let one of them be unhappy, if he can do anything to help her. But there are cases—in short, sir, I have always held it dishonourable to say what might lead an old acquaintance into danger, even though I might not be bound to secrecy."

"But Mr. Menteith is no great friend of yours," said Lionel; "surely regard for him cannot outweigh——"

"I have not a shadow of regard for him now," interrupted Mr. Desmond; "but I had, at one time, a sort of liking for him— we can never quite forget those whom we have pitied and tried to serve—I appeal to your knowledge of your own heart if it is not so.   And the dog seemed grateful once."

"But he has not shown himself so," said Lionel; "he denied his acquaintance with you."

"Ye need not remind me of that, sir!" exclaimed Mr. Desmond, springing suddenly round, and facing Lionel; "no! the villain, he shrank from owning me—but shall my conduct imitate his?   No, no, I have too much honour, I trust, too much chivalry, to act as a craven hound like him might do. He feared me, but I will show him that his suspicions wronged me.   He judged me by himself—he thought that a well-descended Irish gentleman could behave like a low adventurer, such as he is."

"Really, Mr. Desmond, if you have such

a bad opinion of him, I cannot help thinking you are lavishing some superfluous chivalry upon him," said Lionel. " I wonder that, admiring Miss Clyde as you professed to do, you do not wish to hinder her marriage with such a person."

" I do admire her, and I wish ye had her yourself; ah! she reminded me of Donna Iñez—did I tell ye her story ?"

" You did, Mr. Desmond," said Lionel, anxious to avoid a repetition of it ; " and I think, if you will seriously consider the question, you will find that your honour does not require you to keep back any information that may prevent a man like Mr. Menteith being received into such a family as the Clydes."

" I know nothing of the Clydes; and the father, by your own account, must have been something queer, to put himself into Menteith's power. No, if I will not sacrifice my scruples for the sake of a beautiful young woman, is it likely I will for that of a 'stern old parient'? And stern he must be, and selfish too, or he would not urge her to this match. No, no, you must look upon this business as settled, and you must now suffer me to explain to ye a little my theory on the uses of slate. Slate, sir, which is, as yet, but half-appreciated—mines of unexplored treasure lie buried here in these mountains—"

Mr. Desmond turned round, and waved his hand towards the dark background of hills, where the pass of Nant Francon opened its "gloomy jaws."

"Yes, probably," said Lionel, impatient at being led from his subject.

"When we reach my lodgings, where I hope you will dine with me, Mr. Constable, I will show you some of my designs for picture-frames, which I hope to see carried out some day in slate. I am in hopes that Colonel Pennant, who is from home at present, will take up my views when he hears them. They will raise the standard of taste incalculably. The neutral tint of the slate, d'ye see, is eminently adapted to set off some sorts of paintings to advantage —far superior to the glitter of gilding, which is destructive to all delicate colouring. I will just throw before ye a few ideas," and Mr. Desmond launched out into a whole sea of theories upon art and nature. Lionel found that the thread of the discourse had entirely slipped from him, and he was compelled to feign an interest in his companion's remarks until they reached the house. Here he affected to refuse to enter, saying that his business was so urgent he could not afford to lose any more time, unless Mr. Desmond would seriously consider his request.

"I'll take no denial, Mr. Constable; I've not forgotten the time I spent at Railton, and that glorious 121st mess! Fine fellows! —first-rate claret!—and you, the first Railton man I meet, shall not depart without partaking of the poor Welsh fare I can offer ye. If we were in Ould Ireland now, and I had ye at my cousin's castle at Knock-garrymachlinoch, I'd show ye something ye'd never forget. But ye'll come in, surely, and we'll consider what can be done. Sure and I'm sorry for ye, having to give up that charming creature to a red-haired, knock-kneed— ah! that's right—I've got ye fairly under my roof now, so I'll go and order dinner."

They were in the sitting-room by this time, Lionel having consented to follow Mr. Desmond, in the hope of eventually gaining his point.

His host disappeared, but presently returned, and began to unfold and display his designs for picture-frames in slate, which could not, he said, be effectively carried out in any other material.

A long time passed before Lionel could induce Mr. Desmond to talk about anything else; but at last he managed to rivet his attention by saying,

"If I were to tell you that Mr. Menteith had practised a gross deception upon Miss Clyde and her father, should you be induced to expose what you know of his former life?"

"I don't know—I cannot say," returned Mr. Desmond; "besides, how do ye know that I could tell anything bad of him?"

"You have implied as much."

"Well, I'll not deny that I could say what he would not like his lady-love to hear. But ye must tell me, first, what deception he has practised—ye talk in mysteries, and I cannot understand what reason ye have for interfering. Of course, I know your admiration for Miss Clyde, but that's no reason why a man of honour, like ye, should step in between her and another."

"No reason at all," said Lionel, quickly. "Whatever I may feel for Miss Clyde, I am not acting with any view of—there is no understanding between her and myself

—for her own sake, I wish her to be free—
I trust this is clear to you."

Mr. Desmond nodded his head.

"But for some time I have seen that she
was unhappy," said Lionel, "and circumstances have at length made me acquainted
with her peculiar situation."

"But if ye don't tell me the circumstances, I cannot understand the case," said
Mr. Desmond; "and till I understand, I
cannot see why I should put Stephen Menteith in your power."

"I suppose I must tell you the whole,"
said Lionel, after a pause; "though I don't
know how far I am justified in doing so."

And Lionel forthwith began a narration
of the circumstances, so far as he knew
them, concerning the Register marriage of
Stephen Menteith and Beatrice Clyde. Mr
Desmond listened attentively, interrupting
Lionel occasionally by exclamations of surprise and disgust.

"The father must have forced the

daughter into the marriage, no doubt," he said, when the account was concluded; "but why Stephen should have deceived him, and let an illegal ceremony pass, I cannot conceive. What good would it do him? His great point was to secure the girl."

"I am as puzzled as you," said Lionel. "But it might be that he did not really desire an illegal marriage, but was driven into it by Mr. Cartwright's death. That, however, does not alter the fact of his having deceived Mr. Clyde. Of course, so far as Miss Clyde is concerned, it is a matter of rejoicing that the ceremony is not valid, for she is now able to refuse to marry Mr. Menteith. She does refuse; but he immediately comes forward and threatens her father with some dreadful exposure. She is in a most sad and awkward position. She may not waver; but if she keeps firm, she causes misery to herself and all connected with her."

"And from this misery ye think I could save her?" said Mr. Desmond. "Well, maybe I can. I do know a secret that would rather damage Mr. Menteith's plans; and he might keep quiet about Mr. Clyde's affairs if ye could threaten him with it. He's a villain, that's clear, and I don't care a farthing what becomes of him. But there's my honour, d'ye see—the honour of the Desmonds. There never was a Desmond turned spy or informed yet, and they have been tried. Shall Brian Hope be the first to discredit the family reputation? By my faith, and he too, sir, has been tried and tempted before now—when the Carlist camp was pitched before Santacaraqua——"

"Then you absolutely refuse, Mr. Desmond?" said Lionel, impatiently.

"My good sir, have patience. I am considering the matter. I am a man of impulse, but where my honour is at stake I dare not be impulsive. I'd do much to serve you and that queenly beauty—what would I not do in the service of love and beauty? Eyes like stars she had, and hair such as I never saw but once before in my life, and a voice—I hear it even yet!"

Mr. Desmond wandered on, and again and again Lionel strove to bring him back to the point. Several hours of that precious day were wasted before he finally consented to relate what he knew of Stephen Menteith. They had dined then, and were sitting smoking over some whisky punch which Mr. Desmond had brewed. The communication was not made in such laconic terms as Lionel could have desired; but he was glad to get it at any rate, and he wove together the facts Mr. Desmond gave him into a chain of evidence against Mr. Menteith, which would probably prove strong enough to make him alter the course he was pursuing towards the Clydes. It may be thought surprising that Lionel should give credence to a narrative from a man like Mr. Desmond, notoriously given

to exaggeration; but the very difficulty he
had in gaining it made him more inclined
to believe it.   Mr. Desmond was ready
enough with invented anecdotes, and could
have concocted plenty of histories connected
with Stephen Menteith on the spur of the
moment, had not some earnest feeling existed within him, making him hesitate
whether he should tell the whole truth, or
remain entirely silent.   That he had pre-
viously known Stephen, Lionel had never
doubted.   His behaviour on meeting him
at Railton, and on being disowned by him,
bore every mark of reality, and was not
of a kind he would have been likely to
assume; since, whilst betraying his annoyance, he had made visible efforts to restrain
the expression of it.

Mr. Desmond had been a surgeon in the
Royal Navy; and rather more than twenty
years ago, when serving on board the
" Medusa," had first met Stephen Menteith,
who was then a cabin boy in the same ship.

He was known by the name of Stephen Walton, and was an awkward, ill-made, blundering lad of about fifteen. The captain of the "Medusa" was a severe, harsh man—"a perfect savage," said Mr. Desmond, "who flogged the very souls out of the lads who didn't suit him."

"He was the man you mentioned in your lecture when you described the Fow-Chow Islands?" said Lionel.

"The same. I introduced him on purpose, to see how my friend Stephen would like it, and he winced, sir. I saw him, and knew I was not mistaken. He might well wince at the remembrance of the lashes across his back!"

Mr. Desmond went on to say that, when the ship was in the region of the Fow-Chow Islands, three of the men, driven to desperation by the ill-usage of the captain, had deserted. With them was Stephen Walton, whose offence was greater than theirs, inasmuch as, under great provocation, he had

struck his captain.   It was afterwards ascertained that two of the men had died on
one of the islands, another had been caught
at a subsequent period, and had been pun-
ished for his crime ; but no tidings had been
gained of Stephen, and the general opinion
was that he had managed to live concealed
in the Fow-Chow Islands, adopting savage
costume and habits.

   " This was not my private opinion,
though," said Mr. Desmond.   " He was an
intelligent lad, not made to herd with
savages ; and I always believed that if he
were alive he would be heard of again in
civilized life.   Well, I did not stay long in
my profession.   I had a little money left
me—but for that rascally Scotchman I
mentioned to you before, it would have been
more.   Whilst it lasted I lived in London
rather ' on the loose,' as the phrase is ; and
one night, at Jenkins's Rooms—d'ye know
the place?—a sort of debating, speechi-
fying, smoking club—I met Mr. Stephen

figuring away under the name of John
Smith. We recognized each other. He
did not disown me then. I had befriended
him at times—screened him from the captain, and so forth—and I had for him the
feeling one has towards a poor hunted
animal. I never dreamt of betraying him.
I made him feel confidence in me. By my
faith, if he'd kept that confidence, I would
not have betrayed him now."

"How many years was this after his desertion?" asked Lionel; "and how was he
then employed?"

"It might be about three years. He had
altered in the time, but I knew him well
enough. He was living by his wits, doing
copying-work—steady and industrious, it
seemed to me—though rather given to at-
tending Radical meetings and debating
societies — not bad things in their way
—they encourage freedom of thought,
and——"

"Yes, yes," said Lionel. "But can you

follow him up to the time when he entered
Mr. Clyde's service, and was known as
Stephen Menteith ?"

"No. I kept him in sight for about two
years, then I went abroad and lost sight of
him till I saw him that night at Railton,
when I knew him directly. His teeth are
a mark to know him by. I had observed
their shape often."

"Did you know any of his friends?
Could you give me a clue to trace him by?"

"I knew where he lodged, for I had recommended him to some poor distressed
country people of mine; and if I can find
them out, they might know something further of him."

"If we could make out a complete case,"
said Lionel, "and hold over his head the
threat of bringing him to justice as a de-
serter from the Royal Navy, to say nothing
of the other charge, he might be induced
to come to terms. But I should like to
find some other evidence to corroborate

yours, Mr. Desmond, in order to work still more upon his fears."

" I saw an old sailor of the ' Medusa ' in Greenwich Hospital not long ago," said Mr. Desmond, "and I have no doubt he will be able to identify Stephen, and to confirm what I have said about the desertion. By my faith, boy, and I'll go through with it," continued Mr. Desmond, springing from his seat, and waxing doubly Irish, as he always did when he grew emphatic. " Brian Hope Desmond is not the boy to stand shilly-shally, and do his work by halves."

"Then come to London with me," said Lionel, hailing Mr. Desmond's changed mood with delight, " and help me to trace out Mr. Menteith's history."

" With all the pleasure in life. Now that I've told you so much, it concerns my honour to make it good."

"Then let us be off to Bangor at once," said Lionel, " and take the next train to London."

CHAPTER VI.

THE RED-HAIRED CLERK.

LEAVING Lionel and Mr. Desmond to pursue their inquiries, it may be well to look back some fifteen years, to the time when Stephen Walton was living in London, " by his wits," as Mr. Desmond had said ; though there was nothing in his conduct to justify the application of that phrase to him, in the sense in which it is frequently understood. Stephen lived by his wits, but without descending to cunning tricks or shifty devices.

Though in this story he has not hitherto appeared in a very estimable or amiable light, there were, at the period referred to,

many elements of good in his character.
He was capable of great patience, industry,
and self-denial; he had much energy,
endurance, and strength in resisting ordinary forms of temptation; he was actuated
upon the whole by a desire to do his duty;
he was free from any hankering after low
vice, any taste for coarse pleasure; and
though the wish to push himself on in the
world, and to exercise to the utmost his
excellent abilities to his own profit, was
paramount within him, he had no intention
of benefiting himself to the disadvantage of
others, or of knocking over his fellow-passengers by the way. Whether, when
tempted, he might prove scrupulous, remained to be tried.

Stephen had never had any fancy for a
sea-faring life—the unkindness of some
relatives, to whose care he had been entrusted at an early age, his parents having
died in his infancy, had driven him to run
away from home; and in such circumstan-

ces the sea is the grand resource that pre-
sents itself to a boy's mind.

But he had always hated it; the duties
of his calling required qualities totally different from his; bodily dexterity, hardihood,
an exterior promising strength, and securing
in itself almost a guarantee for bravery,
would have availed him far more than the
subtle, calculating intellect which distinguished him even as a lad. His distaste
was increased by the jeers and galling sneers
to which he was exposed by his awkwardness, his mean proportions, his frequent
absence of mind, and his want of social
qualifications.

The daring act he had at last committed,
and by which he had drawn upon himself a
risk that would haunt him to his dying day,
had raised him in the minds of the crew to
a higher pitch than he had before occupied;
and there was hardly a man on board who
would not have screened rather than betrayed him, had circumstances brought the
lad into his power.

But Stephen did not know this, and he was continually tormented by the dread of meeting one of his old ship-mates—he was far from imagining that his conduct had been deemed praiseworthy. He had been incited to it by a rare access of passion, which he had since bewailed with the bitter repentance of a cautious, seldom-roused nature; he was suspicious, and believed that the love of gain would overbalance in the minds of his former comrades any remnant of good-nature for him; and he was aware that the irritated captain had offered a reward for his apprehension.

Thus, even from Mr. Desmond, who had befriended him, he had shrunk in reality; he did not, indeed, anticipate that that gentleman would deliver him up for an inconsiderable sum of money, but still he felt it irksome to be exposed to the notice of one who held him in his power, and who might be induced, by a thousand transitory motives, to cast him off. It was a relief when Mr. Desmond had gone ; and after his departure Stephen conceived a scheme, which would, he thought, double his chances of concealment, and, at the same time, further the ambitious projects he had begun to entertain.

The virtues and the faults of Stephen were rather such as are supposed to belong to mature years than to youth ; but there was one exception—his master-passion was an inordinate, almost childish vanity, that led him into weaknesses and errors inconsistent with the clear judgment and solid sense an older man might have envied, which he exercised on all matters where this powerful feeling did not come into play.

This vanity was none the less absorbing because there was little in his person or circumstances likely to foster it. It took, indeed, most frequently the form of suffering. The want of anything noble and attractive in his exterior was a constant source

of severe pain and gnawing envy to him;
whilst his low origin, and the plebeian name
he had adopted as a measure of safety, filled
him with a continual sense of inferiority.
He desired to raise himself in the social
scale; and he imagined that the cognomen
of John Smith would be a bar to his
obtaining the respect and consideration that
might be granted to a more imposing name.
Childish as this may appear, it was a matter
of serious import to him. He was not de-
void of a certain kind of imagination—that
which springs from the contemplation of
self in every possible attitude, but which is
utterly incapable of entering largely into
the thoughts and feelings of others; and
many a time, during the abstracted fits that
had excited ridicule on board the "Medusa,"
he had been building castles, where he figured
as a man of eminence, consulted and honoured by the wise and great, and even—so
daring were the boy's visions—smiled on by
the beautiful.

N 2

But the name of John Smith was destructive of all romance of this kind ; a John Smith might indeed make a fortune, but he could never fill exactly the post Stephen desired to gain; he might certainly be respected amongst mercantile men, but he would not be distinguished from the hundreds of rich John Smiths in the world. He dare not return to his old name of Walton—the fear of discovery was too strong upon him ; but there was no reason why he should not again change his appellation—casting aside the one he had chosen for its commonness, and assuming a better-sounding designation. By thus doing, he reflected that he should also complicate any efforts that should be made to trace him out.

He resolved, after some deliberation, to call himself Stephen Menteith, retaining his own Christian name, to which he clung with a kind of superstition. He thought the combination produced an important, pleasing effect; whilst Menteith was not, he fancied, fine and romantic enough to make any one suspect that it might not belong to a hard-working young clerk, compelled, perhaps, by the declining fortunes of a respectable family, to seek his livelihood in a subordinate position.

He had no fear of being challenged by relations; those who had treated him un-kindly were either dead, or had vanished into distant lands; and he was not aware that he possessed any others. The only person who could be considered in the light of a connection was a man whom he had encountered since his return to England, and whom he had recognised as a visitor and remote cousin of the people with whom he had lived. This man, Richard Parker, was not likely to betray his change of name. He was, though considerably older than Stephen, much less firm and resolute in disposition, and could be easily led by fine promises, or even through pure laziness, to agree to anything the latter might require. He had already benefited Stephen by getting him work; and it was on the occasion of entering into a situation procured for him by Parker that Stephen determined to adopt his new name. The alteration could be effected without much trouble; for the few persons who had known him as John Smith might be readily cast off, on his transition to a more regular and profitable mode of life.

At the same time he changed his lodgings, leaving the poor Irishwoman to whom Mr. Desmond had introduced him, and trusting that she would not inquire further about him.

But in this he was mistaken; there were human beings in the world actuated by notions widely different from those for which he, with his suspicious temper and calculating disposition, gave them credit; and the Irishwoman, to whom, after his fashion, he had been kind—casting up her accounts for her, and teaching one of her ragged, impish boys to read—possessed all the gratitude to which her country-people lay claim. Though her lodger concealed from her his new abode, she found him out, not, however, betraying her knowledge, until Stephen, partly from confinement, and from overtasking his brain, fell ill, when she burst in upon him, and nursed him through a fever. He paid her with outward attentions, and, after this, never failed in bestowing upon her such little benefits as were in his power; but he inwardly cursed her officiousness, and wished that she had left him to the tender mercies of his new landlady.

Peggy Ryan was not a woman to thrust herself where she was not needed—she had the tact to know that Mr. Menteith, as the young clerk had begun to be called, desired to have as few reminders as possible of the time when John Smith, a half-starved lad, had been sheltered under her roof; and, with the spirit of a duchess, she drew back from the notice unwillingly given. But the fact that she knew him—that she could at any moment declare to the world that his name was not Menteith, or had not always been Menteith, remained behind, an annoyance to Stephen whenever it was remembered.

Meantime, he got on in the world, and, after passing about two years in the office to which he had been recommended by Richard Parker, he obtained, through one of his new friends—he had several, for he was assiduous in cultivating friendships that might be useful to him—an introduction into the counting-house of Messrs. Clyde & Co., which he entered as a junior clerk, but with a salary far exceeding any he had formerly received, and with the hope of rising to a higher post.

He had now arrived at a standing-point which satisfied him for the present. The house of Clyde was well-known to him by fame, and it was precisely the kind of establishment with which he had longed to be connected. The firm drove a considerable business in South America, and Stephen, whether his residence in the sunny Fow-Chow Islands had given him a taste for a tropical life, or that he liked the idea of the responsibility of a distant agency—formed, almost from the moment of his entering the house, the ambitious wish of some day superintending this branch of the concern.

His acuteness soon enabled him to discover that so much profit was not made of the South American connection as might be made; and he dreamt many a dream—far more practical in detail than the old shipboard ones—in which he saw himself conducting this portion of the business, and raising himself to the condition of one of the merchant princes of the New World.

Whilst Stephen rigidly fulfilled the duties of his situation, and gained rapidly in the good opinion of his employers, he neglected

no means of improving his mind. He not
only devoted his leisure to reading and
study, but he spent part of his earnings in
obtaining the instruction necessary to qualify
him for filling his hoped-for future position
of gentleman. He frequented debating
clubs, belonged to literary societies, &c.—
every species of association that has been
invented to give young men an opportunity
of educating themselves; and he probably
bore away as much advantage as was ever
derived from such sources.

There must have been an innate love of
refinement about him, for, with all this, he
sedulously attended to his manners, speech,
and dress, copying, as far as he could, the
habits, and even adopting the modes of thinking, of those above him in the social scale.

He certainly succeeded in escaping vul-
garity, and he acquired a facility of language
only too striking to be natural. He lived
with great prudence, almost with parsimony,
and showed little inclination for even the

innocent amusements of youth. His grand relaxation was an hour's idle musing, when he represented to himself the details of the future he hoped to attain.

More than two years had passed since his entering Mr. Clyde's employment, when he was sent one day by the head clerk with an important message to that gentleman, who was away at his house some miles from town. The place was not far from the Thames, and Stephen took his way by steam-boat. It was a brilliant June day, and the banks of the river wore their gayest clothing. Stephen, as he sat apart on deck enjoying the change from the stifling atmosphere he had left, drinking in the delicious air and sunshine, and revelling in the luxuriance of nature, with the strong animal sense of pleasure that combined so strangely with his self-denying habits, gave himself up to one of the day-dreams that formed the only romance in the midst of his prosaic existence.

He imagined a time when he should be rich and powerful, and act his part in the world as a respected, honoured man; he pictured to himself the hardly won leisure that would alternate with his active life, as adorned with every possible delight that nature could give.

He was a true Epicurean in his fancies, though a stern Stoic in his practice; and sunny skies, shady groves, gorgeous flowers, splendid furniture, and luxurious dishes floated before his mind's eye, in his wished-for Paradise, whilst the charms of society were not wanting.   More than this, a beautiful form ever hovered near him in these visions, and the music of love sounded in his ears.

Stephen's admiration for beauty was intense, and was intimately connected with his mortification at the want of it in his own person ; it was mere material beauty that he prized ; he could not even see that which belongs to expression, but to that

which addresses itself to the eye alone he
was keenly alive. Yet with all his admiration for beautiful women, he never contem-
plated or longed for any career of flirtation
or empty love-making. He always looked
forward to leading a life that should be
thoroughly staid and respectable, and a wife
appeared a necessary adjunct to such a
scheme. So, in the home he imagined to
himself, a wife lived and moved—a wife
both lovely and loving.

Amidst these aspirations, a sense sometimes came across him that he was not fitted
to inspire love—that he was no suitable
mate for the enchanting being of his imagination. But what of that? He knew that
in actual life beauty seldom weds beauty,
and that women are not naturally impressed
like men by personal advantages. He was
far above the weakness, it may be here
mentioned, of seeking to conceal his defects,
or to convert them into beauties by any
quack means: no infallible receipts for dye-

ing his hair found favour in his eyes—no conspicuous fopperies of fashion caught his attention. He was clean and precise to an extreme in his dress, but the beholder was never struck by an incongruity between the fineness of the clothes and the plainness of the wearer. He did not trust, and never intended to trust, to the attractions of his person, but he had the vanity to think that his other gifts might make his outward semblance altogether forgotten. He would have given many of these prized qualities for the sake of a handsome, winning form; but as that could not be, he must make the best of what he had. Eloquent speech he had heard was a ready way to a woman's heart, even with the disadvantage of an unmusical voice; and eloquence, or what he fancied eloquence, he carefully studied. He arrived at the belief that he might, in the end, by dint of great tact, and by the attractive manners he hoped to acquire, obtain an influence and make an impression

far beyond anything that can be achieved
by an ordinary handsome man. Yet with
all this confidence, his keen sensitiveness as
to the remarks of others upon his appearance remained, and seemed to imply a
secret distrust.

In the midst of his medley of thought
about bonds, investments, southern skies,
glancing waters, flowers, women, and love,
he was disturbed by the stoppage of the
steamer at the pier where he was to land.

In a moment he became again the cool,
practical clerk, and during his walk to Mr.
Clyde's house confined his attention to a
review of what he was to say to his master.

Mr. Clyde received him in a small breakfast-room, heard his message, and listened
to the clear explanation of the case he
humbly offered. His answer was soon given ;
and then observing the young man's half-
inquiring, half-admiring gaze cast around,
his furtive glance, through the partially-
closed Venetians, upon the green lawn and
glittering shrubberies, he said :

"You have never been here before, I think, Mr. Menteith? If you like to stay and have a look at the conservatories and grounds, you will be able to do so, and yet get back before post time."

Stephen thanked him with elaborate courtesy, and Mr. Clyde then preceded him through a glass door that opened upon a verandah.

"You'll find your way over the place yourself," he said; "I am on the point of going with Mrs. Clyde and my little girl to Chiswick—it is a fête-day, you know."

Almost as he spoke, a lady and child, both dressed with extreme elegance, and in the height of fashion, entered the verandah by another door.

The lady was beautiful as one of the creatures of Stephen's dreams, and still in the bloom of womanhood; yet her face was too languid to please him, and she lifted her eyebrows, as she saw him, in a kind of depreciating surprise that repelled him. The

little girl was also beautiful—slender, and
dark-eyed, with a complexion white and
smooth as delicate ivory, bright, red lips,
and a clear pink flush on each softly-
rounded cheek.

"This is Mr. Menteith—one of my
clerks, my dear," said Mr. Clyde, in explanation of Stephen's appearance; "he does not
often get a breath of country air, so I have
asked him to look through the grounds."

"Very well," said Mrs. Clyde, as she acknowledged the clerk's bow by a listless
movement of the head. "I thought I heard
the carriage—is it not ready?"

"Ah!—I had forgotten—I counter-
manded the order, thinking I might be
detained some time; but I will see about
it," and Mr. Clyde moved into the hall.

Stephen, left with the haughty lady, and
the inquisitive little girl, who stared at him
with her large, liquid eyes, felt rather em-
barrassed. Though he could talk well
enough with men, he had not yet acquired

the ease and fluency which he had placed before himself as the ultimate result of his efforts in his intercourse with the other sex, and he did not know whether to stop and make some further remark, or to go down the steps that led to the lawn.

Mrs. Clyde decided the matter for him.

"If you have finished your business with Mr. Clyde, you need not wait," she said; "you will find a gardener round there," and she pointed to the conservatories.

Stephen bowed once more, and walked stiffly down the steps.

"Beatrice, my child," he heard in the lady's voice, as he slowly wandered along the path below the verandah, "do not run into the sun—my darling, how often have I cautioned you! What should I do if you were to lose your complexion, sweet? Would you," in a rather lower tone, "like to be freckled like that ugly young man?"

Stephen walked on faster—of course she thought him ugly—there was nothing wonderful in that—but somehow the criticism from such beautiful lips, and in that charming place, so formed to revive the fancies he had been indulging, annoyed him more than he could have supposed possible. The contrast struck him so forcibly between himself and the inhabitants of this abode—he felt himself uglier, meaner, awkwarder than ever—his faith in himself sustained a shock —could it be that he should ever be fitted to feel at home in the scenes, lovelier than this, that he had been imagining?—could he ever hope to mingle on terms of equality with women beautiful and disdainful as the wife of his employer?

Unheeding where he went, instead of turning towards the conservatories, he entered a shady walk bordered by evergreens, and screened on one side by some towering horse-chestnut trees. Presently he heard voices, and he became aware that he was walking along a path, at only a short distance from the house, and that mother and

o 2

child, tired, perhaps, of waiting for the
carriage, had descended into a cool garden-
plot, shaded by an end of the building, and
just visible to him through the trees.
Stephen's hearing was acute as that of a
savage, and it had been sharpened during
his stay amongst the Fow-Chowites.

"He looked very hot and tired, mamma,"
he heard in the little girl's voice; "will
Roberts give him any fruit?"

"Roberts wants my early peaches and
nectarines for a different purpose," said
Mrs. Clyde; "I daresay he will give him
some strawberries, if he wishes for them."

"May I tell him to give him some,
mamma?"

"Nonsense, Beatrice; why do you
trouble yourself about this young man?
And you are crumpling your mantle, my
dear. Come here—you will be an object
before we arrive, and you know I like my
child to look like a beautiful little lady.
Ah! here is papa—is the carriage ready,
Edward?"

" Yes, come along—what have you done with my clerk ? " said Mr. Clyde.

" Oh ! I told him where the conservatories were—I suppose you did not wish me to do more in the way of entertaining such a person. And I hate looking at such hideous people."

" He is not handsome, certainly ; but he has a shrewd, sensible face."

" It would give me the dismals if I had him before me for a long time," said Mrs. Clyde ; " such a very plain, marked face, and so freckled and brick-dusty, and the most hateful red hair. I believe he squinted, too—at any rate, his little eyes had a horrid look. And then, his mean little figure."

" He has plenty in him, nevertheless, and will get on."

" I don't dispute that, in the way of business--he has a sort of ' turn again Whittington ' look about him. I suppose crooked legs and red hair don't hinder people from growing rich. But whatever he may do, he will never get on in society with such an air and figure."

" Why, Alice, I have heard you admire some very plain men," said Mr. Clyde, good-humouredly.

"Oh! I can put up with irregular features, when there is distinguished style— you know I consider your friend, Mr. Elwin, a fascinating ugly man; but that is quite different—I cannot bear ugly people who are insignificant and common also."

"Mamma, when shall we go?" asked little Beatrice, impatiently; and Mrs. Clyde dropped the subject of Stephen's looks, and walked towards the house, in front of which the carriage waited.

Stephen had heard every word—he might have moved away, but a bitter longing to hear the worst rooted him to the spot; and when the voices had died away, and the sound of carriage wheels rattling over the gravel had ceased, he still remained in the green avenue, flinging himself on the turf with an abandonment to which he rarely gave way. He was in that mood of concentrated passion which seldom attacked him, and which had driven him once in his life to a hasty deed, ever after repented. There was no scope for present action, or he might have been tempted to do something equally rash.

Mrs. Clyde had mocked him and scorned him—treated him with supercilious indifference to his face, and severe comments behind his back. It mattered not that he perceived her to be a shallow, silly woman —her dictum as to his unfitness for distinction in the world affected him none the less. He might have powers and perseverance beyond her skill to distinguish—he believed that he had, but he burned with feverish impatience to make her aware of them; he thirsted to compel her to own that he, the red-haired, insignificant clerk, could hold his own amongst the people who formed her world—nay, that he could tower above them by his talents, and the force of his will to attract.

To compel Mrs. Clyde to retract her judgment—to mortify her—to revenge himself upon her disdain—formed henceforth a part of the aspiring plan that Stephen laid before himself.

He stayed on the grass for some time, yielding to his sense of injury, and weaving wild schemes of vengeance; but suddenly remembering that his business did not allow much delay, he started up, determining to see what he could of the lady's luxurious home.

In his present frame of mind every indication of wealth, and device of pleasure, gave him a pang. He asked himself why he, whose capacity for enjoyment was so vast, should have been born to a sordid life—why beauty and refinement had not surrounded his infancy and childhood? To his distorted fancy it even seemed as if, in such a case, his meagre, stunted frame would

have ripened to more symmetrical proportions, and that the careful tending bestowed
upon the children of luxury would have
softened his hard features and cleared his
dingy complexion.

Despite, however, these morbid ideas, he
carried on an intelligent discussion with the
gardener; he never despised any kind of
information—a knowledge of the names and
properties of plants might be useful to him
some time; the methods of forcing, the
recent improvements in hot-houses, the way
of transplanting trees—all might some day
furnish matter for conversation, and add to
his means of impressing people with an idea
of his general cleverness.

He returned to town, as he went, by
boat; and this day, which had already been
productive of such unwonted excitement,
was not fated to close without bringing
him something more in the shape of an
adventure.

He was sitting away from the other

passengers, for he did not see any of a class whose acquaintance might be profitable to him, when an elderly man in sailor's clothes passed him. Something in this man's face attracted his notice, and at the same time impelled him to conceal his own as much as he could, which was, indeed, always his instinctive feeling at the sight of nautical costume. The sailor walked past him two or three times, and at length spoke. Stephen recognized him at once as a man called Benjamin Hicks, who had served on board the "Medusa." It was too late to retreat— the sailor had already mentioned his true name, Stephen Walton, and he determined to put the best face upon the matter. He avoided conversation for the present as much as possible, saying there was too much noise to talk comfortably; and when the voyage was over, and Hicks had followed him from the landing-place, he took him aside, and confided to him that he had changed his name, begging him no longer to address him by his former one, unless indeed he, the old acquaintance, had any design of giving him up to justice.

Benjamin Hicks, an honest, straightforward seaman, was aghast at the mere notion of such a proceeding; and, curious to see what was the present condition of him whom he had known as a silent, awkward lad, but whose rebellion had turned indifference to sympathy, insisted on walking with him towards his destination.

Stephen received the amicable advances of the man with apparent cordiality; but he avoided telling him the name he had assumed, and trusted to getting rid of him by some happy chance before reaching the place of business. In the street, however, leading to the warehouses of the firm, they were met by a fellow-clerk of Stephen's, who hailed him with,

"Hey, Menteith! you must make haste. Mr. Ingle is in a fine state about that letter. It's just post time, and he has to write it yet."

" I'll be there in a moment," said Stephen ;
and, turning to his companion, he added—

"I can't stay with you, Hicks, I'm too busy."

"So you're called Menteith ?   Well, we
must meet again, youngster, and have a
jaw.   Where do you hang out ?"

Stephen, afraid of offending the man, and
having no excuse ready, was obliged to invite him to his lodgings—after which, Benjamin, saying, " All right !   I'll come soon
and see you, my boy," turned his steps in
another direction.

This encounter was highly disagreeable
to Stephen; and though, after a few interviews in which he practised his most con-
ciliatory manners, he became assured that
his old shipmate was not deep enough, or
base enough, to take advantage of him, he
was greatly relieved when Benjamin Hicks
started on another voyage.

Before he was likely to be again in England Stephen took care to change his lodgings.

CHAPTER VII.

A HARD BARGAIN.

LATE one evening Mr. Clyde was sitting in a small private room adjoining his counting-house, in which he had lately spent much time, remaining in town long after the usual hours of business.

He sat now, with his head resting on his hand, absorbed in thought, and the lines on his brow, and the vacillating expression of his mouth, spoke of some mental conflict and painful hesitation that he had gone through.

Mr. Clyde was of a speculative turn, and as the other partners of the firm were emphatically "sleeping partners," he had much in his power. Of late he had used this power to the utmost, and had been drawn into difficulties, under pressure of which he had been tempted to commit an action whose possible consequences he now dreaded, whilst his remembrance of it agitated him with remorse. By signing the name of another person, a sum of money had fallen into his hands, sufficient to save the credit of the house, which had been in danger; and he had also been thus enabled to conceal that danger from his partners.

Nothing but his weak fear of the world's opinion would have driven Mr. Clyde into such a course, for he was naturally a conscientious man; and now that the deed was done he fancied that he would have forfeited much to be able to recall it. He fully intended to restore the money he had appropriated, and trusted to do so in a short space of time; but, meanwhile, he could not silence the reproaches of his own heart, nor turn away his eyes from the fact that his error, if ever discovered, would bear the ugly name of forgery.

As he was thus musing the door opened, and Stephen Menteith entered. It was now five or six years since he had visited Mr. Clyde's house on that brilliant June day, and heard the depreciating remarks of Mrs. Clyde, which he had never forgotten or forgiven. During these years his advancement had been steady. He held at this time a responsible situation in the house. He had a good salary, and he had made full use of his enlarged means of self-education. His address was improved, and if he had failed in acquiring the demeanour of a true gentleman, he had managed to steer clear of the rocks and shoals of gentism.

" Menteith!— I thought you had gone home!" exclaimed Mr. Clyde.

" No, sir; I purposely waited, that I might have some private conversation with you," said Stephen, gravely.

Mr. Clyde's fears were always alive, and the suspicion that Stephen had found out his late irregular dealing struck him at once.

He was not wrong. Stephen, ever on the look-out for something that might turn to his advantage—ever longing to obtain means of mortifying and humbling Mrs. Clyde —had noticed for some time the harassed state of his employer's mind. He had suspected some flaw in the affairs of the firm, and had turned his attention to a subject somewhat apart from his immediate duties. Every step lately taken by Mr. Clyde he had traced; he knew the unwarrantable, dangerous act he had committed—he, and he alone—and he had now the power in his hands of consigning his master to the legal consequences of his guilt.

In very respectful terms he informed Mr. Clyde of the facts that had come to his knowledge. He made no accusation—ventured upon no blame; he simply repeated his statement, concluding by saying:

"Now, sir, what can I do? I trust—nay,

I am sure, no one else as yet suspects this; but if they should do so, and you are brought to answer for it, I may be accused of having concealed the transaction."

Mr. Clyde made no answer, but the deprecating expression of his face was pitiable.

"Sir," continued Stephen, "you have been a kind master to me, and I have no wish to bring you to ruin; but I must look out for myself. If I consent to keep this secret, I must have enough benefit to make up to me for the risk of being afterwards suspected of being mixed up with your proceedings. My character, sir, is all I have in the world."

"I know it," said Mr. Clyde; "but indeed you exaggerate your risk. This—these unfortunate circumstances I have been driven into, will soon pass. What I have done I have done so carefully, that it is a marvel how you have made the discovery, and exceedingly improbable that another person should repeat it; and even if so, I don't see that you would be compromised."

"Be that as it may," said Stephen, still respectfully, but with much decision —" I cannot promise not to reveal what I know without some conditions. I will not deny, sir, that I have ambition ; and, casting aside all consideration of your conduct in a business or moral point of view, I think my own inter-est demands that I should not let slip this chance of improving my condition. I speak frankly, sir ; I don't presume to question the right or wrong of what you have done—I only say that if I agree to keep silence, I must have some stronger motive for silence than the mere wish to spare you."

" Of course—of course," began Mr. Clyde; "I am aware that I am in your power—I assure you my fault will soon be repaired ; meanwhile, anything that I can do——"

"Your fault, sir, will never be so far re-paired that I shall not have the means of exposing you," interrupted Stephen. " It will be your interest to make such terms as shall bind up your honour and mine together."

"What do you mean?" asked Mr. Clyde, turning very pale, but drawing himself up with some dignity. He was a proud man, and he did not relish the notion of his own honour and that of his clerk being spoken of in the same sentence.

"I mean," returned Stephen, with a quiet consciousness of power in his tone, "that if I were a partner in the house, and, still more, if I were connected with you by a private tie, it would be my interest to conceal for ever from the world that you had at any time acted in a way not strictly honourable."

"A partner in the house!—that is a great thing to ask, and does not depend upon me alone to grant."

"Your influence, sir, is great; if you promise to exert it with the other members of the firm, I am sure of what I ask."

"But such an unheard of rise!—a mere clerk to become at once a partner! Indeed, Menteith, such a proceeding would rouse the very suspicions we wish to avert."

"Which *you* wish to avert, sir.   However, if you refuse, my course is plain—I must declare what will ruin you."

" Stay !—do not be hasty — let us consider," said the unhappy and bewildered man.

" Any reasonable length of time you desire for consideration I will grant," said Stephen, now fully assuming the tone of superiority ; " but I don't think you quite understand my proposition ; it was not that you should at once elevate me to the rank of a partner—that would excite wonder.   I only ask, at present, that you should send me to Rio, to inquire, as your agent, into the state of the business there.   It is not well managed, sir, and in a few months I doubt not that I shall be able to give you information that will make you dismiss Mr. Barlow from the post he holds.   I then expect that it will be made over to me, and that by degrees you will obtain the consent of the other members of the firm to my· having a share of the business."

"This is not so unreasonable," said Mr. Clyde, catching at the prospect of the removal from the country of the man who knew his secret; "I will see what can be done."

"You have not considered the remaining term," pursued Stephen; "I said, also, if I were bound to you by a private tie."

"I cannot understand what you mean by such a sentence—"

"Yet you have a daughter, sir—give her to me, and my father-in-law's credit and honour will be mine to guard."

"Menteith, are you mad?" exclaimed Mr. Clyde, quivering with powerless rage; "was such an audacious demand ever made before?"

"The position in which we stand to each other is novel, sir, yet the arrangement has been heard of before. Whittington married his master's daughter," said Stephen, recollecting Mrs. Clyde's careless allusion to his "turn again, Whittington," look; "but do not answer at once—you can consider which you prefer—to have a son-in-law who will further your concerns, who will increase—I can confidently promise it —the · returns of the American business tenfold—or to appear before the world as——"

"Hush!—hush!—you need not tell me the alternative; but, Mr. Menteith, you are pitiless!"

Stephen smiled—a cold, pitiless smile it was—and yet the smooth respect in his voice was undiminished as he said,

"I am aware that I am not the sort of person you would choose as a husband for Miss Clyde, but, unless I greatly deceive myself, you would not, in future, have to be ashamed of me. She will be maintained in luxury as great, if not greater, than that she has been accustomed to; and in a distant land it will not be known that I am not naturally her equal in rank. Nor will you and Mrs. Clyde be subjected to the sight of—

"Mrs. Clyde!—my wife! how will she ever be induced to—how will she ever be reconciled to such a scheme—with all her views for Beatrice—and such a child as she is! Do you know that she is only fifteen? How can we trust her out of our sight, in a foreign country—a trying climate—and with one who is a stranger to her, whom she has no cause to like or respect?—the sacrifice is monstrous!"

"I know Miss Clyde's age, and I had not formed the idea of withdrawing her from her mother's care at present—nor do I wish you to bestow your daughter upon me, *apparently*, in my now humble condition."

"Then what do you mean?—an engagement?"

"Not precisely. On the few occasions when I have seen Miss Clyde, it has struck me that she promises to be very beautiful —she will doubtless meet wooers more attractive than I am, and she might choose

to take affairs into her own hands. No, sir
—your daughter must be bound to me by
marriage—a marriage as secret and private
as you can wish—but she must be bound
to me by a tie no caprice of hers can break.
Immediately after the ceremony, which I
would not wish to take place till just before
my departure for Rio, I will leave your
daughter in your hands for some years.
When I have attained the position I desire,
I will return—openly woo her, and receive
her openly from you. There will then be
nothing so very strange in your bestowing
her upon me."

"But what a position !—my poor child !
—a girl bound by a secret tie, appearing
free to the world ! Mr. Menteith, you don't
know what you ask."

"Indeed, sir, I do; but I trust to you
to impress upon her a sense of her peculiar
position, and to keep her heart free from
anything that may interfere with her
duty to me."

"It is incredible!—one would think you were influenced by some enmity towards me, to propose such galling terms!—such a fate for my child!"

"Pardon me, sir, you view the case in a one-sided manner—you cannot expect me to see anything so very lamentable in Miss Clyde's fate."

"I cannot understand it; if she were older—if you had seen more of her—if your feelings were engaged—but it cannot be possible that you are in love with her?"

Stephen smiled again. "I am not in love—my motives are connected with my own advancement."

"And if I give her to a man who feels no affection for her, how do I know what misery may befall her?"

"Though I am not in love," answered Stephen, "I am prepared, when the time comes, to feel a sincere attachment to your daughter; and you need have no fears that I shall ever fail in my duty towards her,

or cease to be proud of and grateful to
the beautiful creature who has brought
me my good fortune."

The blood rushed to Mr. Clyde's face
—he could have knocked Stephen down
for what appeared to him the insolence of
his speech, but fear restrained him.

"You talk of fortune," he said; "I will
strip myself to give you wealth, if you
will leave me my daughter."

"Mr. Clyde, if I had wanted money I
would have asked for it. I have asked
you for what I do want—I must have the
position I should hold as your son-in-law
and your partner."

"You may be my partner—you may
hold an equal position—you may win a
richer wife."

"Sir, I wish to have Miss Clyde for my
wife, and no one else. This is no hastily-
formed desire—I have long been aspiring,
and this scheme, if carried out, will fulfil
all my aims."

"It is strange!—unheard of!" murmured Mr. Clyde, in a perplexed manner.

"Take time to consider, sir—I have said all I have to say—I leave you to decide;" and Stephen withdrew.

Mr. Clyde's mind was a chaos. It is needless to dwell upon the hundred vicissitudes of feeling through which he passed. Circumstances were too strong for him; he could not struggle successfully against Stephen's power. He was an affectionate father, but dread of exposure to the world, of bearing the doom he had invoked by his own fault, was stronger within him than parental feeling, and he decided to give up his daughter to her strange suitor, if she could be induced to make the sacrifice.

The indignation of Mrs. Clyde, when the subject was mentioned to her, knew no bounds. She was greatly attached to her husband, yet her reproaches were more stinging for that very reason. It

was the first time of her being made
aware Mr. Clyde had acted in a dishonourable manner, and she blamed him with
a vehemence that owed more to rage and
disappointment at the consequences springing from his guilt than to moral dis-
approval. She declared positively that
her lovely child should never be given up
to such a hideous monster, as she termed
Stephen, whose physical defects were more
repugnant to her than his humble origin.

In desperation Mr. Clyde appealed to
Beatrice.

The girl was called in from her ramble
in the grounds, from her youthful fancies,
from her pleasant, dreamy idleness, to
decide the grand question of her life.

As she entered, with a light, springy
step, her father almost groaned.

Beatrice at this time was not beautiful;
still less could she be called a pretty girl.
But those who had seen her radiant childhood could forgive Mrs. Clyde for the rap-

tures she indulged in about her daughter's
charms, and prognosticate that the pale,
small face, and thin, lanky figure, would
bloom into riper beauty. At present the
eyes seemed too large for the other features,
the arms too long for the frame, and the
weight of dark hair, coiled round the head,
too great for the slender neck to support.

Full of ardour and impulse, affectionate
in disposition, devotedly attached to her
father, who had himself taken pains to draw
forth her intellect, and to counteract the
frivolity encouraged by her mother—and
strongly imbued with a spirit of Pagan
heroism, contracted from the study of an-
cient history, there can be little doubt as
to Beatrice's answer to the questions proposed to her.

She trembled, and her lips grew pale, as
Mr. Clyde narrated the terrible circumstances in which he was placed. The shock was
tremendous—the loss of her faith in him
through the unveiling of a guilt she could

never have imagined! But it was in her power to save him from degradation, and she did not hesitate.

"Beatrice! my child! my darling!" exclaimed Mrs. Clyde, "you shall not do this! I forbid you, ungrateful girl, after all my cares for you—all my hopes! You shall not submit to your unnatural father's caprice."

"Alice, it is no caprice. God knows, I shrink, as you do, from giving her up to this man. But the alternative is ruin. If I refuse I shall be poor and dishonoured—your fine projects for Beatrice, whatever they may be, will not be carried out—you will have to live in obscurity, whilst I—the law will condemn me—I will use its lightest name, Alice—I shall be exiled."

A burst of tears from Mrs. Clyde, upon whom now first descended the full sense of the magnitude of her husband's danger, interrupted further speech for the present, and when she recovered her mood was changed.

She implored Beatrice to save them from beggary and disgrace; and when Beatrice again declared her willingness, she turned upon her with her disappointed hopes, and hurled new reproaches at her husband.

"This is the end of all your speculations! I thought you were such a man of business as the world never saw! Oh! that I had never met you! Little did I think, when you carried me away as a bride, and all my guardian's guests said we were the handsomest couple they had ever seen, that it would come to this—and the merchant I preferred to—well, I had better offers—would turn out as bad as any swindler, and destroy the prospects of his only child!"

"Alice, spare me! Beatrice cannot now respect me as she did; but at least do not show her that you despise me. But for you, I would starve. I would bear all that might be said against me. Nay, as it is, banishment and the scorn of the world are preferable to this—to hear your reproaches, and

lose your affection. I will go and tell Menteith that I have decided."

"No!—no! Edward, you shall not! I
will not lose you. But surely we might
escape, save some of our money, and go
where this man could never find us?"

"Never! My character would be lost
for ever. I would rather stand a public
trial than sneak off in that way. I should
indeed be a common swindler, as you called
me."

"Then Beatrice must save you. But
what an idea!" said Mrs. Clyde, with a
change of tone. "Who would have thought
the creature cared for her?—dared to raise
his eyes to her?—the ugly, red-haired wretch!"

"He does not care for her in that way,
but he is ambitious, and fancies it would
advance him to have her as his wife; but
he does not love her—how should he, child
as she is?"

"I don't know—I had two offers before I
was seventeen."

"It is all the better," said Beatrice, with vehemence; "as I shall certainly always hate him, for the way he has treated my father."

"Beatrice, you must not speak so wildly," said Mr. Clyde; "remember, if you make this sacrifice, you must endeavour to look upon Mr. Menteith as your husband—to do your duty by him."

"But you said we should be parted for many years?"

"Yes; but the time must come when you will live together," returned Mr. Clyde, gravely; "and upon your conduct and thoughts in the meantime your future happiness or misery will depend. And we must not be prejudiced against him, Beatrice—he has some excellent qualities."

"As if she could learn to care for a wretch like that!" said Mrs. Clyde; "I declare, Mr. Clyde, you put me out of patience—no, no, my darling, at least they should let you hate him as much as you like, and forget him as much as you can, when he is out of sight."

Mr. Clyde pressed his hands to his forehead; his responsibilities as a father—his
love as a husband—his dread of the world
—his still-remaining, conscientious feeling—
a thousand other thoughts and sensations—
crowded upon him, and crushed him to the
dust. He broke off the scene abruptly, and
quitted the room.

Many more ensued—all painful—tragical,
but for the ludicrous element which was
infused by the frivolities of Mrs. Clyde. The
result is known—advantage was taken of
the consent of the victim, who, unconscious
of the vast extent of the sacrifice she was
making—supported by the proud belief of
acting heroically, worthy of a Grecian
daughter, yet intuitively felt that, by her
own deed, she was trampling under foot all
those sweet hopes, romantic longings for
sympathy, that of late had risen in her
girlish dreams.

It was arranged by Mr. Clyde and Stephen
that the ceremony should be performed at a

Register Office, on the morning of the day that Stephen was to sail for South America. He was to settle all the preliminaries, Mr. Clyde gladly yielding to him the management of an affair so distasteful to himself.

Stephen determined that the marriage should take place at the Register Office of the district to which he belonged, and he took care to have the proper notice posted up three weeks before the appointed time, and every requisite formality attended to.

The morning arrived—the seventh of September—Stephen had only returned from Bristol late the night before, and, at an early hour, he repaired to the office of St. Benedict's. The clerk, who was no other than his friend, Richard Parker, greeted him with some perplexing intelligence that had just reached him. Mr. Cartwright, the Registrar, had died suddenly—who was to perform the ceremony?

There was no time to seek any other office—the ship by which Stephen was to

sail would start in a few hours—in half-an-
hour from the present time Mr. Clyde and
his daughter would arrive. In this ex-
tremity Stephen hit upon a plan, to which
he induced the clerk, for the sake of old
friendship, and other more weighty considerations, to consent—he was to personate
Mr. Cartwright, who had never been seen
by Mr. Clyde. It would be easy enough to
imitate his signature, and, for the sake of
avoiding future inquiries, the entry might
be ante-dated, so that it would appear as if the
ceremony had taken place on the day before
Mr. Cartwright's death.

Mr. Clyde and Beatrice arrived, unsuspi-
cious of anything wrong; the false marriage
took place, and Stephen felt satisfied that his
hold on the bride was secure. Pale and sad
she looked in the dingy office on that misty
September morning ; but Stephen, as he
shook hands with her for the first time when
he left her at the door, felt no regrets. He
departed—fulfilled his promises as regarded

the business—was shortly received into partnership, and wrote from time to time to Mr. Clyde, as if he considered himself the husband of Beatrice.

Mr. Clyde, a short time after Stephen had left England, replaced the money he had appropriated, and his fraud remained undiscovered; but that Stephen knew it was a never-forgotten mortification—whilst at the same time his anxieties for Beatrice went on increasing. He was honourably desirous to keep, as Stephen had desired him, her heart free from anything that might interfere with her after-duty; and the admiration her beauty excited, and the flatteries of her mother, kept him in constant alarm on this head, making him sometimes harsh and suspicious. Stephen, throughout the eight years of his absence, had no communication with Beatrice beyond a few formal messages, and sending her the year before his arrival a chain and locket, which he begged her to wear then, as a mark of her relation to him.

It was the letter accompanying this present that had caused Beatrice so much agitation on that memorable night of the charade-rehearsal. It had been put into her hands just as she was starting, and she had been reading it with rebellious indignation, when Lionel had approached her in the window. By her father's desire she had answered it; but her reply, written on the day of Captain Denbigh's proposal, had contained merely a few words of curt civility.

The indifference with which Stephen had considered Beatrice was amply avenged by the passionate love he conceived for her on his return to England—a love which made it almost torment to be bound to one who was to him as a block of ice; whilst at the same time the notion of her freeing herself from the bond filled him with rage. His schemes had succeeded. He was a rich, prosperous man; but all was unheeded in the might of his desire to obtain Beatrice's heart. Had he not been so much absorbed

in her, he might have felt some disappointment at finding how very poor had been his
revenge upon Mrs. Clyde. True, the painful
situation common to the whole family had
told upon her; the anxiety and the misery
that had harassed her husband and daughter
had reflected themselves in some sort upon
her, rendering her a querulous invalid; but
her light nature had retained no deep impression, sustained no overwhelming mortification; and when Stephen had returned
to marry Beatrice in due form, and with
sufficient *eclât*, she had found consolation
amidst milliners and dress-makers, and had
become reconciled to the idea of having him
for a son-in-law, so far as to look upon his
red hair as a misfortune and not as a crime.

As for Beatrice, during these intervening
eight years, she had daily become more vividly conscious of what she had renounced.
She had naturally strong desires for happiness, and a keen sense of enjoyment; and in
binding herself to a man with whom she could

not hope to find a single sympathy, and whose
behaviour to her father had checked even
the possibility of respect, she felt she had
blighted her whole life.

Her mother's murmurings had only made
the bitterness of her lot more difficult to
endure; and she had been led into incon-
sistencies — perhaps blameable levities and
reckless snatching at shadowy pleasures—
simply from the wish to escape thought and
forget her wretchedness.   Then one had
come who learnt to love her truly and tenderly—whom she might have loved; and if
she had not discouraged his advances so
chillingly as she should have done—if she
had suffered him to suspect feelings she had no
right to entertain—judge her not too harshly.

Every moment of forgetfulness was paid
for by hours of anguish; every transient
thrill of unwarrantable delight was atoned
for by an aching, tortured heart, wearing
itself out with beating against the prison bars,
and sinking at last into wearied, sullen despair.

CHAPTER VIII.

MEASURE FOR MEASURE.

IT was the evening of Monday, the 28th of November, and everything in Wynthorpe Palace spoke of the grand event of the morrow—the marriage that was expected to take place. Dora and Jessie Lyttelton, together with Amy Constable, had come over to dinner, and were now busy in the drawing-room, making some final preparations, which could not be entrusted to any persons of less refined taste and delicate fingers.

Stephen Menteith hovered near them, ill at ease in his own mind, but veiling his real mood by an appearance of great interest in

their employment, and by offering sugges-
tions, which made him considered an authority in all matters of decoration.

Mrs. Clyde flitted hither and thither—
now up-stairs in Beatrice's dressing-room,
contemplating the magnificent veil and
wreath in which the bride was to make a
sensation next day—now surveying the
breakfast-table below, already set out in
shining array. As for Beatrice, she walked
up and down the drawing-room with an air
that appeared to the expectant bridesmaids
one of supreme indifference, and that made
them think her a greater puzzle than ever.

In reality, Beatrice was oppressed by a
weight of emotions too mingled to analyse.
Stephen's apparent confidence alarmed her
in spite of herself. She was resolved not to
marry him, yet she could not help fearing
that she might not be able to carry out her
resolve. It was so difficult, in the midst of
the stir of preparation that was going forward, to believe there would be no wedding

at all. And even if she were firm, the flight of Richard Parker might make it difficult to prove that the former marriage was null and void; and then, too, there was the dreadful fate impending over her father.

Her father, whose face, grown infinitely more haggard, and visibly aged within the last few days, smote her with self-reproach every time she looked at it. It seemed unnatural and undaughterly to condemn him, in his declining years, to pain and degradation which she might spare him. But yet she could not—no, she dared not, a second time, take vows against her heart and her conscience. And to-night the decision must be spoken. Stephen must receive his final answer. Well, anything would be better than the present state of seeming suspense and living deceit.

Beatrice went up to her father, who was watching, with vague, half-pleased attention, the nimble fingers of Dora and Amy amongst the flowers they were arranging into bouquets, or twining into garlands, seeking, perhaps, to delude himself into the belief that their labours would really be turned to their destined account on the morrow.

"Papa, will you come with me to your study for a little time?"

Beatrice's voice startled her father, as if he had been dreaming; but he rose instantly, and, without saying a word, followed her out of the room.

Stephen looked uneasily after them, but continued a description of a South American creeper he was giving to Janet Sinclair. Dora, Jessie, and Amy drew closer together, and conversed in whispers.

"Miss Clyde is very odd to-night," said Jessie. "I thought she spoke quite authoritatively to her father just now, and he followed her just like a lamb. Poor old gentleman! all this fuss is too much for him."

"That is his step outside; he is coming

back again," said Amy, after a minute or two; "no—he is calling Mrs. Clyde—what are they all about, I wonder?"

"I see no cause for wonder," said Dora; "doubtless, on the last evening, the members of the family wish to be by themselves a little. For my part, I am surprised that we were asked to come at all."

"Oh, I daresay it was on account of the Sinclairs," remarked Jessie; "we are supposed to take care of them."

"Mr. Menteith seems able to do that," returned Dora.

"He is a queer man," said Jessie; "he and Miss Clyde hardly take any notice of each other to-night."

"Miss Clyde always was unlike other people," observed Dora, "and I suppose she always will be. This engagement has been very hasty—people who can leave all their family ties on such short notice, and banish themselves into distant regions, must be peculiarly constituted. Take care, Amy, you are cutting those stalks too short."

"I should think nothing of it," said Amy, unheeding the concluding remark, "if she were really fond of him; but I cannot see anything in him to please her, and she has never seemed to care about him."

"The choice of a flirt is always a matter of wonder," remarked Dora, sententiously. "Pray, did not Miss Clyde appear to like Captain Denbigh, and then refuse him? But I really cannot see why she should not like Mr. Menteith; he is agreeable and gentlemanly. It is only the hurry that I object to."

"He is so unlike any one she has seemed to care anything about before," said Amy; and there was another pause, broken only by remarks about their work.

Suddenly a slight noise was heard in the hall, the door of the room was thrown open, and Mr. Constable announced. Amy flung down her scissors, and flew to meet her brother.

"Oh, Lionel, when did you arrive? Are you come to take me home?"

"No, not yet," answered Lionel, speaking gravely, and bowing to the rest of the party; "I did not expect to find so many people here—I came to see Mr. Menteith."

He went up to Stephen, and said a few words to him in a low voice.

"Certainly," answered Stephen aloud, and the two men left the room together.

The bridesmaids looked at each other in surprise. "I wish we were at home," said Jessie to Dora, "there is something strange going on, I feel sure. What can Lionel Constable want with Mr. Menteith—have you any idea, Amy?"

"No; and I never dreamt of his coming down at all—he has not written for some days, and he never told us he was in Railton last week—I never knew Lionel so mysterious."

"I believe, for my part, that he is in love with Miss Clyde," said Jessie, "and he has

come to quarrel with Mr. Menteith—fight
him, perhaps."

"My dear Jessie, what ideas you have!"
exclaimed Dora; "I believe you pick them
up from the foolish stories Mr. Curzon tells
you. I am sure Mr. Constable is far too
sensible to think of an engaged girl; and
indeed, Amy, I never thought your brother
was so much struck with Miss Clyde as
some people."

"He always admired her very much,"
said Amy.

"Ah! admiration is one thing—esteem
another," returned Dora; "a sensible man
will never love a woman he cannot esteem."

The door again opened, and Beatrice
entered; she was evidently much agitated,
and after looking rather wildly round the
room, she said,

"Ah! Mr. Menteith is not here," and was
turning to go.

"He and another gentleman went out
together," said Janet Sinclair.

Beatrice stood still for a moment, and looked puzzled.

"My brother came a few minutes ago," said Amy, "and wished to speak to Mr. Menteith."

"Ah! at last!" exclaimed Beatrice, and she darted away.

"What can all this mean?" asked Amy.

"It is impossible to say," answered Dora. "Really, Jessie, I begin to think with you, that there is something very strange about this wedding. One thing has struck me several times—there are no friends of the bridegroom's to be present."

"It looks as if he had none," returned Jessie. "And there are no relations of the bride's either, except the Miss Sinclairs."

"Whom we are sadly neglecting," said Dora. "I am quite shocked at our ill-breeding; but, really, the events of this evening drive away all one's usual ideas. Let us join them, and help them with that dreadful wreath they are trying to make."

So the two divisions of bridesmaids amal-
gamated, and the fanciful labours were pursued in ˙common; but a sort of restraint
rested upon all, and many a nervous, wandering glance towards the door, and an
eager listening to any momentary sound in
the hall, betrayed that curiosity was busy.

Beatrice, meanwhile, hurried into the
breakfast-room, where she thought she
would be most likely to meet Mr. Menteith
and Mr. Constable.

They were there. Lionel had apparently
just finished speaking, and Stephen, with
his hands before his face, was leaning
against a table, incapable, as it seemed, of
saying a word. He looked up as Beatrice
entered, displaying a white, frightened face,
and Lionel was starting forward to meet
her, but restraining himself, he only said—

" I am come in time, you see; and I have
discovered something that may make Mr.
Menteith keep your father's secret."

Beatrice uttered an exclamation of relief

and thankfulness, but shuddered instantly as she saw the wild, despairing look Stephen cast upon her. He roused himself quickly, however, threw aside his abject bearing, and with some semblance of dignity said—

"I have not yet declared, Mr. Constable, whether your threat will make me spare Mr. Clyde—and I have not yet heard Miss Clyde's decision."

" You shall hear it without delay," said Beatrice. "It is made already, without reference to you or your threats ; but I wish all to be done in the hearing of my father. Will you come with me to him, both of you ?"

She glanced towards Lionel as she spoke, and he and Stephen followed her at once across the hall to Mr. Clyde's study.

When they entered, a painful scene presented itself. Mrs. Clyde, who had been called in by her husband at the eleventh hour to assist him in working upon Beatrice's feelings, and who had only just learned the complication of embarrassments and griefs which had been agitating the hearts of her husband and daughter during the last week, was crouching on a low easy chair before the fire, weeping violently.

Mr. Clyde, in his usual seat, was leaning back with an air of exhaustion, uttering from time to time faint ejaculations of reproach against some absent person, which had only the effect of increasing his wife's hysterical sobs.

Beatrice advanced into the room pale as marble, and with a forced calmness in her expression. "Papa, I have brought Mr. Menteith, and Mr. Constable has arrived. He knows——"

"Oh! Mr. Constable!" burst in Mrs. Clyde, ceasing her weeping at the name, "can you save us? You are kind and clever, and you used to like Beatrice a little, I think. Oh! save my husband!—prevent that wicked man from tormenting us! I always hated him, and foresaw misery from the moment the sad, unnatural match was proposed. Yes, I even had a presentiment, when first I saw him, that he would do me harm——"

"Hush, hush, mamma!" interrupted Beatrice; "let Mr. Constable explain."

"Beatrice, you have no right to speak—you declare you will not carry on this affair to save your father—wretched, selfish girl!"

Mrs. Clyde's words died off into sobs, and as they became fainter and fainter Lionel began to speak.

"Mr. Clyde, I have found out that Mr. Menteith has a secret which will endanger his prosperity, and his good name, if revealed. I have here proofs," Lionel took out some papers as he spoke, "that the person calling himself Stephen Menteith is really one Stephen Walton, who, twenty years ago, deserted from the Royal Navy. This offence, though under the circumstances not without excuse, exposes him, as he well

knows, to great penalties; and unless he
agrees to terms I shall propose, I positively
declare to him that I will have him brought
to trial.   I have enough evidence against
him, as he cannot deny.   I have here a
deposition taken down from the lips of Mr.
Brian Hope Desmond, surgeon on board
the 'Medusa,' the vessel from which Stephen
Walton deserted.   This gentleman met him
afterwards in London, where he was living
under the name of John Smith; and he
also recognised him in Railton, not long
ago, under his present name and character."

"But is it certain—is there no doubt that
Stephen Walton and Stephen Menteith are
the same?" asked Mr. Clyde, hastily; "the
recognition of one person, after many
years——"

"Mr. Desmond is not the only person
who can speak to the identity of the man,"
said Lionel; "I can show you also the
deposition of Benjamin Hicks, a sailor on
board the 'Medusa' at the time of the de-

sertion—mutiny, rather, for Stephen Walton struck his captain—now a pensioner in
Greenwich Hospital. This man saw Mr.
Menteith many years ago in London, after
he had assumed the name of Menteith. He
had many interviews with him, and knew
that he was in your employ. He is ready
at any moment to swear that Stephen Walton and Stephen Menteith are one and the
same person. Nay, I shall also be able to
produce the evidence of other persons who
knew Stephen Walton in London during
the transition period, when he went by the
name of John Smith—his old Irish landlady
still remembers him."

Mr. Clyde, before Lionel had finished
speaking, was attentively considering the
papers; whilst Stephen all the time remained
motionless, buried, as it seemed, in deep
thought.

The game was lost for him, and yet he
could scarcely own so much even to himself;
he glanced towards Beatrice, who was trying

to pacify her mother. He read a stern determination in her whole bearing, against which he felt he had no power. If she had declared before that she would brave his threats, and refuse to marry him, in spite of what he might bring upon her father, how would it be now? Now, that her father in turn could threaten him? Stephen knew that it was useless to deny the weight of evidence Lionel Constable had collected. His past life had been tracked, step by step, too correctly, for any simple denial of his to avail. At any moment, if he were to proceed to extremities with Mr. Clyde, he might himself be brought up on the charges of mutiny and desertion; and though his conduct on that long-past occasion had been far less blameable than many an action of later years—though extenuating circumstances might be brought forward in his favour—the mere fact of the discovery that he had been a common ship-boy would be enough to overwhelm him with shame.

Whatever might be the result of the trial, the disgrace would be the same—disgrace as dire to him as any he could draw upon Mr. Clyde.

The structure he had spent years of hard labour in raising would be shattered at once—his prospects blighted, and the whole end and aim of his existence snapped off.

And he would gain nothing. Beatrice would never be his—she would only hate him more than ever, as the instrument of evil to her father — even his vengeance would be incomplete. Mr. Clyde's efforts to remedy the wrong he had done would be favourably considered; and the fact that he was accused by the man who had been in his employ for so many years, and who had for so long concealed the crime, would tell forcibly against that man.

Beatrice and Lionel might yet love each other; some day, spite of all his efforts to blast their happiness, they might be united. As he gazed from one to the

other, he felt his powerlessness; though
they scarcely appeared conscious of each
other's presence, there was, he knew, between them, a subtle tie, such as never,
never had existed, nor ever could exist, between Beatrice and himself.

Strive as he might, he could never gain
her—she had slipped from his grasp; and
even the poor vengeance he would have
taken upon her was being snatched away
from him by his rival—the man for whom
he had experienced an instinctive dislike
from the moment of first beholding him.

When Mr. Clyde had read the papers
Lionel had given him he said,

"Then, if these be true, I am no longer
in Stephen Menteith's power?"

"No," said Lionel; "at least, if Mr. Menteith begins proceedings against you, I
shall immediately take steps to bring him
to trial, which I should be sorry to do, as I
confess I have more sympathy with him on
the subject of his behaviour on board the

'Medusa,' than I can feel on any other point."

"I am not surprised at anything he ever did," said Mrs. Clyde, utterly forgetting what a partisan she had been of Stephen's during the last few weeks; "I never had any confidence in Mr. Menteith; you may remember, Edward, I warned you, years ago, that he was a low, designing man."

"Hush, Alice, pray!" said Mr. Clyde; "this demands great consideration—we do not yet know how far this testimony may be depended upon."

"You do right to question it," said Stephen, coming forward, and assuming a rather defiant air; "the statement of a wandering scamp like Mr. Desmond is scarcely to be relied on. I am astonished that a person of Mr. Constable's sagacity should have based his inquiries upon the random stories of an inveterate—liar. All your Railton friends, Mr. Clyde, will assure you that he largely tried their credulity."

"I will not deny," said Lionel, "that Mr. Desmond is a rattling talker, and draws considerably upon his imagination — the stories he tells in society manifestly owe a great deal to his invention; but I could not get him for a long time to tell me any story at all about Mr. Menteith, though he saw, perhaps, that I was in a credulous mood. The reluctant way in which he gave his testimony vouches for its truth, to my mind; and as Mr. Menteith may see, it is written down in grave language, very unlike the careless talk that enlivened Mr. Carleton's supper-table, and also confirmed by an oath. If it does not satisfy Mr. Menteith, the *vivâ voce* evidence which Mr. Desmond is willing to give will satisfy any court of justice. And he does not stand alone, as I said before—his statements are corroborated by those of others."

"I am still bewildered," said Mr. Clyde, rousing himself from a short reverie; "I am at a loss to understand the great interest you take in my affairs, Mr. Constable."

"It is easily understood," said Stephen, bitterly; "Mr. Constable wishes to thrust me out of the way between himself and Miss Clyde."

"You wrong him," exclaimed Beatrice, rising and looking at Stephen with flashing eyes. "After all that has passed, and all that must pass, before I am free, there can be no question of the kind you imply between Mr. Constable and me. It is an insult to him and to me to dream of it—do not interrupt me, Mr. Constable—I will say before my father and mother and Mr. Menteith, that I receive what you have done for me as a pure act of disinterested generosity."

"You have too high an opinion of me," said Lionel, in a low tone. "My motives are not, perhaps, quite so pure as you think; but still I would serve you with my life, without hope of a greater reward than you have just given me."

Beatrice coloured violently, and a sudden

longing came across her to throw aside all
dignity and reserve, and to say to Lionel
exactly what she thought and felt; but a
quick remembrance of the hard ordeal still
before her, chilled every warm impulse,
drove the blood back to her heart, and left
her calm and pale as before.

" Miss Clyde," said Stephen, making a last
hopeless effort—" you have not given me
your final answer ; will you marry me to-
morrow, or pay the penalty of seeing your
father accused of the crime of forgery ?"

Lionel Constable started at the word "forgery," but he commanded his countenance
instantly, and listened to Beatrice's answer.

" I will not marry you," she said; " and if
you still persist in carrying out your threats,
I am willing to bear all you can do."

A loud burst of weeping from Mrs. Clyde
followed this declaration. Every one else
remained silent, except Lionel, who drew
near Beatrice and whispered:

" Right; you have answered wisely and

bravely. He can do nothing that I will not counteract."

Stephen looked from one to the other as they stood opposite him. His eyes glared out from his white face, seeming nearly black from their hollowness, and expressing almost at the same moment intensest love and intensest hate—love for the woman who was defying him, hate for the man who was aiding her to escape from his grasp.

When Mrs. Clyde's hysterical sobs had died away in hollow moaning, Mr. Clyde's voice broke the silence.

" My daughter has decided; but you appear to have forgotten, Mr. Menteith, that your power over me is not quite absolute. If you "—Mr. Clyde hesitated, and his lips trembled with agitation—" if you proceed to extremities, you know what Mr. Constable has said he will do. But he had not then heard the name of my crime—perhaps he will now shrink from any connection with me."

"Never!" said Lionel. "If you will allow me to act—to stand by you like a friend—I will not fail you. Whatever you may have done in past days, I am certain you deserve help now against this. As for you, sir," turning to Stephen—"Mr. Desmond is within two miles of this spot; Mr. Lyttelton, a magistrate, is but across the park—you had better pause in your threats. But I need say no more. I am sure so prudent a man as you are will see that your wisest plan is to make a compromise. Let us hear no accusations on either side—no bringing to light of long-past and repented offences. Consent to make a joint application with Miss Clyde for the annulment of the tie that has linked you together; give me a written assurance, that you will preserve Mr. Clyde's secret as religiously as you have hitherto kept it; and I, on my part, will write as solemn an agreement as you choose, never to breathe a word of what I know of your former life."

Stephen had been far from forgetting that

his power was over, when he had uttered his last threat against Mr. Clyde. He had done it in the futile hope of rousing Beatrice's compassion for her father, and drawing from her some rash promise. He saw clearly now that it was useless to struggle further; even were he to escape the clutches of the law, his reputation would suffer—his story would be blazoned forth. As Lionel had said, his wisest plan was to make a compromise.

He yielded, but with mortification so bitter, disappointment so intense, that exposure to the whole world would scarcely have been greater torment. He felt humbled in the eyes of Beatrice and of her mother, and the sensation to a man of his vanity was agony.

Failure, too, to one who had hitherto been almost uniformly successful, bore an ominous aspect—it seemed as if his good star had forsaken him, never again to shine upon him.

He resolved, however, as far as he could,

to make a virtue of necessity; and in a voice
which trembled a little with hidden passion,
he said—

"It is manifest that I am utterly detested
by Miss Clyde—I see it fully now, though
in my blindness I fancied I might overcome
her aversion; it is impossible, and I will
throw no obstacles in her way.   I am willing, nay, desirous, that she should be free,
and, as Mr. Constable observes, it will be
best to abstain from all accusations, and to
keep all old offences hidden from the world.
I resign Miss Clyde, fully and completely."

Though every one knew that this resigna-
tion was compulsory, no one appeared to
believe it other than a graceful act; and with
much politeness towards each other, Lionel
and Stephen set about arranging the terms
of the written agreement.   No one tri-
umphed openly over the fallen man;
Beatrice, indeed, slightly curled her lip at
his declaration, but there was no other
mark of contempt shown—all were too

deeply impressed with the serious nature of the drama they were enacting; and as for Mrs. Clyde, the speech of Stephen positively imposed upon her, for the moment, as a piece of generosity.

Beatrice, struck by a sudden remembrance, now approached the table where the two men were occupied, and said something in a low voice to Lionel.

" Ah ! " he returned, aloud; " I anticipated this, and it is provided against—Mr. Richard Parker is watched, and he will not leave his present abode without my knowledge, for some time, at any rate; but as Mr. Menteith has declared that he will throw no obstacles in the way of your release, and as Mr. Parker is evidently much under his influence, we must hold him responsible for the clerk's appearance, when required, to be identified as the man who passed himself off as Mr. Cartwright."

" This is rather hard," said Stephen ; " how can I prevent the man's escape ? "

"You may refuse to assist him, at any rate—and you have power over him. I suppose you are aware that he is liable to be brought up for forging Mr. Cartwright's signature? Not, I fancy, that anyone would wish to press this, and ruin a man who has borne a good character, and only erred perhaps through weakness, and the persuasion of a stronger nature," and Lionel looked at Mr. Clyde.

"Oh! no, no, certainly not," he answered to the look; "let all be kept as quiet as possible."

"If, however, Mr. Parker cannot be forthcoming in any other way," pursued Lionel, "it may be necessary to act against him. Surely you can induce him to remain and appear at the proper time, Mr. Menteith, in order to avoid the other peril?"

Stephen bowed.

"I shall insert, then, in the agreement a clause which makes you responsible for the appearance of Richard Parker, upon which my keeping my share of the agreement depends."

"Upon my word, Mr. Constable, you know how to drive a hard bargain," said Stephen, in a less stilted manner than usual.

"It is an art in which you need not take a lesson from me, I think," returned Lionel; whilst Mr. Clyde fixed upon Stephen a look which plainly said,

"There was a time when you, too, were pitiless."

The papers were now drawn up and formally signed; and it was agreed that as soon as possible the legal proceedings should be entered upon to obtain a declaration of nullity of marriage between Stephen and Beatrice.

In the meanwhile, as probably much time must elapse before the case could be heard, Mr. Clyde made no objection to Stephen's returning to Rio, and conducting affairs there as before.

Stephen, after the *éclaircissement*, would

have no wish to continue in partnership
with Mr. Clyde and the other sleeping
member of the firm, and he now declared
his readiness to enter speedily upon arrangements for his withdrawal from the business.
But, for the present, matters would remain
as they were, and Stephen would have some
months before him in which to look about
him, and prepare for carrying his energies
and the capital he had realized to another
market. Though he had lost Beatrice, and
failed in his darling scheme, he had yet arrived at a position in life which he would
scarcely have attained by other means than
those chance had placed within his power
eight years ago, and of which he had taken
such determined advantage.

Doubtless, in future this knowledge would
be consolatory to him ; but at present he
fancied he was indifferent to everything except getting away, and escaping from the
eyes of Beatrice. Though she scarcely
looked towards him, her glances seemed to

burn him. The love that would have made him still desire to linger in her presence was overmastered by the humiliation of knowing himself outwitted, and feeling himself ridiculous in her sight.

Preparations were quickly made for conveying him to the station, where he meant to take the next train to London ; and in the meantime Lionel left the party in the study and went to the drawing-room, intending to take Amy away as soon as possible from a house which would shortly become a scene of wonder and confusion.

He was assailed with questions from the bridesmaids, who were all sitting in a very subdued and silent state when he entered, pondering upon the cause of their being neglected. But before he had given any plausible answers Beatrice walked into the room. There was a fixed, determined look in her dark eyes, and a decided air in her whole bearing that commanded immediate attention.

"I have come," she said, "to tell you that your services will not be required to-morrow as bridesmaids. There will be no wedding."

Looks of surprise and dismay were turned upon her.

"Yes," she continued, "the marriage is at an end—*for ever!* Mr. Menteith is going away, and you will probably never see him again. As for me—I cannot explain now —I am sorry for having deceived you—led you to expect"—her voice trembled a little "you will know all some day." She shook hands with Jessie and Dora, saying, with a half smile,

"You will publish the news at home. There is no need to send notes of apology."

When they were gone she kissed Amy, and her self-possession quite deserted her as she pressed the bewildered girl in her arms.

"Amy! — Amy! — I love you! Don't think hardly of me when you know——"

Amy replied only by a burst of tears and a convulsive hug.

Beatrice sat down utterly exhausted and quivering in every nerve, scarcely heeding that Lionel left the room without saying good night. He returned, however, in a moment, and seeing that the Sinclairs were engaged in eager conversation at the other end of the room, he drew near Beatrice, and bending low, took her hand in his. She looked up at him—her face pale as death, her eyes wild and hollow, her lips trembling: he was not less moved, and for some seconds they gazed, without speaking, into each other's faces.

"You will not fail," he said at last— "you will bear bravely all that must come."

"I will," answered Beatrice.

There was another pause.

"I must not linger," said Lionel; "and we may not meet again, perhaps—but you will trust me—feel that I am a friend?"

"My best friend," she replied, with emphasis; "but go now."

"Yes—I must go—I must take Amy

home, and send that good fellow Desmond a line that all is right. We shall travel together to London to-morrow. No one will know he has been here, except the people at the Station Hôtel."

Beatrice was not heeding his words, and he knew not why he said them, except as an excuse for gazing a moment longer on the pale worn face on which he felt he now looked for the last time, for many months, perhaps years. His look was bringing back the blood to Beatrice's cheeks—her eyes were filling with a new light.

" Go," she whispered faintly—" you must not stay."

Lionel raised himself from his stooping attitude. Their hands met in one long convulsive clasp, and they parted.

Lionel rejoined Amy in the hall, and the brother and sister walked homewards.

Just after they had passed the Lodge gates they heard a dog-cart rattle down the drive, and Amy, looking back, could see, by the faint moonlight, the huddled-up figure of a man who sat by the driver. It was Stephen Menteith, on his way to the railway station.

Beatrice remained motionless for some time after Lionel had left her, but at last she remembered that her work for the night was not yet over, and she rose to set about it. Calling Janet and Emma, she made them sit down at a writing-table, whilst she dictated to them a number of notes that were to be sent out early in the morning, to stop the different guests who had been invited to the wedding. This business finished, she went to seek her mother, who was bemoaning her hard fate to Larkins; regretting that the beautiful dresses which were to have appeared on the morrow would now remain in obscurity, and in the same breath storming against Beatrice for having concealed from her that she meant to break off the marriage.

Larkins, bewildered by the strange turn

of affairs, hailed the appearance of Beatrice with delight, as it enabled her to escape, and discuss with her fellow-servants the cause of the sudden departure of the bride-groom elect; but Beatrice stopped her for a minute, to give directions about the convey-ance of the notes, and various other orders which were now necessary.

Beatrice knew that there was no one but herself to make any exertion, for both her father and mother were too much over-powered to know what course to pursue.

"I am sure I wonder, Beatrice, you can come to me, after all that has happened," said Mrs. Clyde; "you to appear before a Divorce Court! I know all about it—I made your father explain it—you will bring us all to shame—oh! to think of such an end to all my prospects for you!"

"Mamma, mamma!—you used to wish that dreadful marriage had never taken place —now that it is proved false, why do you reproach me?"

"I am glad, certainly," began Mrs. Clyde; "he is a common-looking, low creature, and you know I could never bear his hair and eyes; but after all was settled, and I had made up my mind to it! To turn round at the very last moment—and every one wondering! And all the wreaths, which were so lovely! And then that dreadful Divorce Court—to think that a daughter of mine should be so talked about! I shall never face the world again, I know; and you will be ruined for life—who will think anything of you now?"

So Mrs. Clyde rambled on, and Beatrice listened with forced patience, and strove to pacify her as well as she could. Hours passed before she could leave her mother, and then she had to go through an exciting scene with her father.

It was one o'clock in the morning when she went to her own room, where her bridal dress and wreath were still laid out, in readiness for the next day. Larkins had been too busy talking to put them away, and Beatrice, crushing all together in one heap, which she thrust into a closet out of her sight, prepared rapidly for rest, and threw herself on her bed, too worn-out to think, or even to realize what had happened.

CHAPTER IX.

THE RIDDLE SOLVED.

BEATRICE's first sensation when she awoke next morning was one of inexpressible relief. The dreaded twenty-ninth of November had dawned, but it would not be her bridal day. Stephen was gone, and his power to torment her had vanished. Now, for the first time for many long years, she dared to believe in the possibility of happiness. Life was no more considered as a burthen to be endured, but as a gift to be wisely and nobly used, and also richly enjoyed.

But before long other thoughts arose to disturb the first, sweet, waking moments of

conscious freedom; that freedom must be
secured by the sacrifice of many a cherished
feeling. Womanly delicacy and reserve
must be rudely shaken, and the privacy of
domestic life cast aside; her story must be
published to the world, and subjected to the
comments and misconstructions which pre-
judice and rash judgment would surely call
forth—a severe trial to most women, and
not the less so to Beatrice because she
was naturally frank and free from prudish
scruples. Innate modesty was as strong
within her as it was within the breasts of
those who most condemned her lightness
and frivolity. She shrank for a moment in
thought, but her spirit rose again directly to
meet the inevitable. To purchase freedom,
no sacrifice could be too great—nothing too
terrible to brave!

Beatrice rose and went about her duties
during the day; there was much to be done,
and for a time excitement kept her up. She
had to entertain the Sinclairs, who were now

anxious to depart, feeling themselves in the way, but who could not leave till the next day. Various arrangements, which had been made for the wedding, had to be unmade, and the burthen of all fell upon Beatrice. Her mother had shut herself up in her dressing-room with a violent attack of nervous headache; her father was altogether unstrung by the agitation he had passed through, and was incapable of any kind of business. The servants were full of curiosity and importance—anxious to leave the house on one pretext or other, for the sake of talking over the strange affair with the tradespeople, and appearing to know a great deal more about it than they really did. Mrs. Williams, the housekeeper, was so cross at the untimely end which had overtaken her grand preparations, that no one dared speak to her—in short, the household was thoroughly out of sorts; and Beatrice, knowing that she was the cause of the disorder and bewilderment, felt bound to do all that depended upon her as patiently and carefully as possible. But it was wonderful how much more easy it was to bear every cross—to meet with energy every difficulty—now that she could carry about with her the blessed consciousness that she was no longer under a hated thraldom. She resolved that, after this day, no relic should remain to remind her of the state of bondage against which she had so long fruitlessly chafed; and, taking Stephen's chain and locket, which she had the night before unclasped from her neck for the last time, and, adding the other trinkets which she had been compelled to receive from him, she made the whole into a parcel, which she begged her father to despatch to him immediately.

She now most dreaded meeting her neighbours, and undergoing the scrutiny of their curious eyes; but she was spared the pain of this infliction—for the day after the Sinclairs had gone away, on attempting to get up, she found herself too ill to leave her bed, and several weeks of low, nervous fever showed the effects of excitement and reaction upon even her strong constitution.

After her recovery change of air was recommended, and the Clydes soon left Wynthorpe for a more southern part of England, and ultimately went over to the Continent.

Meanwhile, gossip was not idle : on the day which should have been that of the wedding, Railton and Wynthorpe were seized with a calling mania.

There was a large gathering at the house of the Carletons, for they were supposed to know as much of Miss Clyde as any people in the neighbourhood, and to be as able to form a shrewd guess as to the cause of the sudden breaking off of the marriage.

Dora and Jessie Lyttelton were amongst the visitors; they had driven over to Railton, finding it impossible, Jessie said, to stay quietly at home on the day when they had expected to be so differently engaged.

" I don't care a straw for the wedding," she said, " but it is too bad to be done out of the dance."

"Too bad indeed!" said Mr. Curzon, who, with the other officers, had been invited for the evening; "we have lost our two gallops and three waltzes."

"You would not have had them with me if we had been there," said Jessie, "I never promised so many."

"Jessie," said Dora, "Mrs. Carleton cannot believe that Miss Clyde came in and told us herself that the affair was at an end."

"Indeed she did," said Jessie; "and she looked as cool as possible, I thought, and announced the news just as she might have told us she wanted to get up a charade. Just the same high and mighty manner."

"Well, I never knew anything so odd, but Miss Clyde always had plenty of confidence," said Mrs. Carleton; "I remember her on the night of the charades——"

"And how she used to sing 'the

Canteeneer,'" added Dora; "however, I am sure her coolness is most enviable; few people could carry through such a thing as this—breaking off an engagement on the eve of marriage!"

"Few people would break one off on the eve of marriage," said Mrs. Carleton; "but has no one any idea of the cause of her behaviour?"

"We came to you to be enlightened," said Colonel Morley.

"I assure you I am quite in the dark; but, Dora, Jessie, surely you might be able to suggest something?"

"Well," said Jessie, "my private opinion is that Lionel Constable has more to do with it than any one; he came in very mysteriously, and asked for Mr. Menteith."

"And was he in the house when Miss Clyde announced that the wedding was off?"

"Yes—in the room—I am positive they are in love with each other, and that he did not propose till too late."

"A fearful warning for bachelors!" said Colonel Morley.

"Jessie, you are talking nonsense," said Dora, severely; "and how can we tell who broke off the engagement? It might be Mr. Menteith's doing, not Miss Clyde's."

"He found out, perhaps, that she had flirted with Mr. Constable," said Mrs. Carleton; "you know, she always appeared rather pleased with him."

"I wish she had married him instead of entangling herself with the other man," said Mr. Carleton, who had just entered the room.

"For my part," said Colonel Morley, "I am glad that Miss Clyde is to remain Miss Clyde still; she is far too pleasant a puzzle to be swamped into matrimony. My worst wish to her is that she may find victims to flirt with for the next ten years. She does them no harm—indeed, I am convinced that she formed Denbigh's character."

"Oh, Colonel Morley! what a shocking

fate to wish any woman!" exclaimed Dora.

"I don't know—it would be rather a jolly life, I think," said Jessie; "only in ten years she will be quite old."

"Is Lionel Constable at his mother's house?" asked Mr. Carleton.

"No," returned Dora; "for we called this morning to see Amy, and found he had already gone. He only arrived last night, and went straight from the station to the Palace."

"And what does Mrs. Constable say about his sudden appearance and disappearance?"

"Only that Lionel came on business of Mr. Clyde's," said Jessie; "whether she knows more, I can't say, for she is very reserved when she chooses, and she looked so grave, I thought she must be vexed at something."

"She is sorry, perhaps, that Miss Clyde has turned out so ill," said Mrs. Carleton; "she used rather to like her."

"Oh! you women!" said Mr. Carleton; "why do you say a girl has turned out ill because, finding she cannot care for a man, she refuses to marry him at the last? I think she has shown a great deal of moral courage, and if the man had any sense he would thank her for it."

"Oh! come now," said Mr. Ashton, who had hitherto listened in silence; "one does not like to see a fellow thrown over, you know, even though he may not seem good enough for her. A fellow must feel so sold."

"What has become of the forlorn one?" asked Colonel Morley.

"He went away last night," said Dora; "Amy Constable saw him driving off in a dog-cart."

"Most prosaic mode of conveyance for a disappointed lover!" remarked Colonel Morley. "I wonder you ladies can get up any sympathy for him."

"Well, of all the unaccountable stories I ever heard, this is the most so," said Mrs.

Carleton; "what do you think of it, Mrs. Baker?" addressing a lady who had not joined in the conversation.

"I have been thinking of all the wasted preparations," she answered; "I know what it is to have a wedding in the house, and to have all the fuss, and no wedding must be aggravating."

"And I am thinking," said Mr. Carleton, solemnly, "of the bridesmaids' wreaths. What will be done with them? I saw one, and I know how pretty they would have looked."

"What nonsense, Edmund!" said his wife; "I am sure this matter is too serious for one to think of such trifling things as bridesmaids' wreaths."

"I declare," said Dora, "I could not sleep last night for thinking of the horrible situation for a girl to place herself in—I don't think I could have survived such a thing myself—being made the subject of such remarks and conjectures!"

" Who is Mr. Menteith, I should like to know?" said Colonel Morley; "in spite of his irreproachable manner, I cannot believe that he is really a gentleman."

" And no one knows anything of his friends," said Jessie; "I fancy sometimes that the Clydes have heard something they don't like about his connections."

"Not unlikely," said Mr. Carleton; "but I cannot conceive why Mr. Clyde ever allowed an engagement between his daughter and a man he knew nothing about."

" And I am sure Mr. Menteith always appeared to me quite a gentleman," observed Mrs. Carleton.

" He was never thoroughly at ease," said Colonel Morley.

" He was too confoundedly jealous to be at ease," said Mr. Ashton; "how I have seen his eyes glare if one attempted to be merely civil to Miss Clyde. Positively, he made one feel uncomfortable—afraid of causing mischief."

" I observed you drew back a little after his arrival," said Colonel Morley; " it was most discreet and kind—to avoid the possibility of Miss Clyde's being too civil to you, and so occasioning a quarrel."

" Oh ! now, you need not chaff a fellow in that way," said Mr. Ashton; " I meant nothing, upon my honour; Miss Clyde is a very fine girl, but——"

" You need not explain," said Mr. Carleton; " we will all acquit you of the charge of meaning anything serious."

On this same morning, the character and motives of Beatrice Clyde were being discussed at the Laurels with scarcely less animation than at Railton. Amy was defending her friend as well as she could, and Mrs. Constable was now condemning, now excusing her, and secretly wondering, the while, what real connection Lionel had with the whole affair. Mrs. Lyttelton and Mrs. Newton were present, both highly shocked at what had occurred.

"If Helen had turned round in that way the night before her wedding," said Mrs. Lyttelton, "I should have scolded and reasoned her out of her folly. A girl *must* know her own mind before affairs have gone to such lengths—at least, I know my children would have been afraid to behave in such a way. It is quite a scandal! Think how it harms a girl to be talked about! Who will think of marrying Miss Clyde now?"

"Mrs. Clyde enjoys such very poor health," said Mrs. Newton, "that she has not strength, I suppose, to contend against a decided young person like Miss Clyde. Certainly, it is a dreadful thing; as I said to Mr. Newton this morning, during the number of years you have been in the church, such an event has never occurred. I should think such an affair will get into the county papers."

"How horrid!" said Amy—"to be put in as a young lady not a hundred miles from Railton! Poor Miss Clyde!—yet I do think she was right, if she could not love Mr. Menteith."

"Only she ought to have known before," said Mrs. Constable. "I fear a young woman who can allow an affair to go so far, and then break it off when all has been made so public, can have very little feminine delicacy and proper shrinking from observation."

"Miss Clyde never did care much for people's remarks," said Amy; "but I admired her for it—it seemed so strong-minded."

"I trust you will never show yourself strong-minded in the same way, Amy," said her mother. "However, whilst we blame Miss Clyde, we must not forget that we don't know everything. There may be circumstances to excuse even what she has done."

"She has not been worse than the young lady who jilted Mr. Collingwood," said Amy.

"Well, I confess I think there is something behind," said Mrs. Lyttelton—"judging from what the girls have told me."

It was a long time before curiosity at Wynthorpe and Railton was satisfied on the subject of Beatrice Clyde. After she had left the neighbourhood, however, people grew tired of talking about her; and as in the spring Mr. Clyde gave up the Palace, and it was let in due time to other tenants, it appeared as if the family had vanished utterly into space, and would never more be heard of.

But at the close of the year the whole community was startled by the sight in the *Times* of a case before Sir Cresswell Cresswell, headed "Menteith *versus* Menteith." The riddle was solved at last—the clue gained to most of Beatrice's odd actions and apparent caprices; and though many still blamed her, others could find in the singularity of her position an excuse for all her flightiness and bitterness. Several things concerning her still remained in obscurity. The cause for her originally consenting to marry Mr.

Menteith never appeared ; nor was the way in which she had obtained the knowledge of her actual freedom clearly explained. The whole affair did not occupy many lines, and concluded with the statement that a declaration had been obtained of "nullity of marriage between the parties, Stephen Menteith and Beatrice Clyde."

CHAPTER X.

WON AT LAST.

IT was a bright morning in April, just a year and a half after the occurrence with which the last chapter closed. The sun was shining on the fortifications of Gibraltar, and glittering over the sea, where numerous boats were plying to and fro, and the tall funnel of the P. & O. Company's steam-ship " Pera," rising black and distinct against the pale blue sky.

The view from the heights that spring sheer and straight above the quaint old town was brilliant and picturesque. Land and sea were bathed in dazzling sunshine, whilst the day was not sufficiently advanced for vivid colouring to be lost in glare and haze. Beatrice Clyde, mounted on a sturdy Spanish mule, was enjoying the novelty of the scene, and gazing intently and with some curiosity upon the steamer which was that day to convey her towards England, after an absence of nearly eighteen months.

The Clydes had been wandering through great part of Europe; and after spending the winter in Spain, had arrived at Gibraltar a few days since, to await the homeward-bound Indian mail.

Beatrice had already explored the whole place, and on this last morning had succeeded in persuading her father to accompany her to the top of the cliff.

Mr. Clyde now looked much older than his years. Suffering had left lines upon his face, which could never be effaced; and though still active in his habits, and refusing to own any feeling of fatigue from the exertion of riding up the hill, he was visibly

much more feeble, and had far more of the
old man about him, than in the days when
he and Beatrice used to ride into Railton
together.

Beatrice, unlike her father, had improved.
Her face was bright and blooming, her
clear, pale complexion had gained a soft
pink flush with the fresh air and the exercise, which she had enjoyed abundantly of
late—and her look, at once of animation
and tranquil happiness, gave a new charm
to her features. It is true, there were depths
of feeling in her eyes, and a shadowed expression about her brow, that told of past
experiences, and indicated that her life had
not always been calm and joyous. The
gladness which illumined her face was not
that of earliest youth, and her beauty had
not the soft roundness of girlhood—it was
the beauty of a woman who has felt and
lived. The expression was that of one who
has known both joy and sorrow, and who
has immense capabilities of entering vividly
into both.

Beatrice had indeed undergone much tumult and suffering during the time before her case was heard in the Divorce Court.

How she lived through the weary months —how she bore the caprices and complainings of her mother, listening patiently to the carelessly uttered words which stabbed her cruelly to the heart, she could never afterwards clearly remember. The whole affair seemed like an evil dream, that she would gladly banish from her memory.

Perhaps nothing could have supported her but a comparison of her present situation with the former time, when she had writhed in bondage, and when freedom from the tie that bound her to Stephen would have appeared the height of happiness.

At last it was over. She had survived the shame of publicity, agonizing to any woman, galling to one of even Beatrice's high spirit and defiant nature. Her name had died away on the public tongue, and she was, in reality, free.

She had seen Stephen once after the trial.
He had said good-bye to her and her father
before starting for North America, where
he was about to begin business in one of
the commercial towns. He was well off as
regarded money, and his skill and energy
were great enough to ensure his success,
whilst the stain which his behaviour about
the false marriage might have left upon his
character in England was not likely to mar
his prospects in the New World. He
vanishes now utterly from this history, but
his future may be easily enough predicted.
He will rise to wealth and good position.
He may, perhaps in after years, for the sake
of worldly advantage, marry some rich,
well-connected woman ; but he can never
again experience the frantic passion he felt
for Beatrice Clyde. The ambition of his
early years, which animated all his hopes
and efforts, may still be gratified ; but there
will be a hidden scar upon his heart, a
secret bitterness engrafted upon his nature,

which will remain to the end of his days.

The clerk, Richard Parker, disappeared from England at about the same time as Stephen, and, it was supposed, had been taken under his protection. The man had appeared at the trial, but probably fearing that prosecution for forgery, which no one was really inclined to undertake, knowing that at any rate his credit and respectability had sustained a shock, he had been glad to withdraw himself as soon as possible from his native country, and to begin a new career under the auspices of his old friend.

Beatrice had never seen Lionel Constable since the evening of that memorable twenty-ninth of November, between two and three years ago ; but after the declaration of her freedom he had written to her, and had had an interview with her father. At that time she had been too much shocked by all that had passed to dare to indulge any thoughts of Lionel as her future husband — there would have been an indelicacy in entering

upon any new engagement until her strange
story had ceased to be much remembered;
and she refused, and Lionel did not urge
her, to consider herself regularly betrothed
to him.

But each of them had an innate conviction of the other's truth; and though they
did not correspond, Lionel always learned
from Mr. Clyde what was befalling Beatrice.

Mr. Clyde could not make any objection
to the affair; indeed, it was gratifying to
his mortified, wounded feelings to find that
a man of honour and good name, who knew
the whole truth about himself, could seek
an alliance with his daughter.

"Papa," said Beatrice, turning to her
father, after a prolonged gaze at the view
before her, "do you see those people coming up the hill?—they must be from the
steamer, I think—three gentlemen and two
ladies."

"Yes, I see," returned Mr. Clyde; "they
are Indian passengers, I suppose. One of

the men has a regular Indian hat on."

"With the red turban sort of thing fastened round it? Yes—it looks funny here. They seem to be afraid of the sun even in Europe. Another of them has a white covering on his helmet-like hat—I don't know which looks most outlandish."

"The ladies, too, look rather forlorn," remarked Mr. Clyde.

"So shall I, I daresay, by the time we reach Southampton," said Beatrice. "Life on board ship is destructive to everything like elegance or even order in dress. But shall we go down, papa? I should rather like to meet those people—the man in the red turban reminds me of some one I have seen."

Mr. Clyde assented, and in another moment they were descending the hill. As they passed the party from the steamer, Beatrice indulged in as long a stare as she dared towards the man in the red silk *puggree*. He was occupied in arranging the bridle of the mule ridden by the lady next him, and she could not see his face very clearly. But just as he was close to Beatrice, he looked up for an instant, and as he saw her face he gave a slight start, almost of recognition.

She had gone from his sight, however, before he could confirm his impression, and Beatrice had not looked at him after he had raised his head. She turned to her father, as soon as they were out of hearing, and said,

" I do believe that was Captain Denbigh. What I saw of the face, and the whole air, reminded me so of him—only such a very fierce beard makes a great difference."

" I never thought of him," answered Mr. Clyde; " but the man seemed to me like some one I had known."

No further remarks passed on the subject; but after they had gone on board the "Pera" in the afternoon, Beatrice was very anxious to ascertain the names of her fellow-passengers. The business of coaling was only just over, and the deck was still rather black and dirty; but it looked less comfortless than the interior of the vessel, where the carpets had been rolled up, and the furniture covered with dingy cloths, to prevent the insidious encroachments of coal-dust. In the cabins, too, the ports were still closed for the same reason. So Beatrice, after seeing her mother, as comfortable as circumstances permitted, on one of the couches in the saloon, established herself on deck, watching the passengers who had been on shore, as they approached the steamer in boats.

The party she had met on the hill had not yet returned, and the hour which the captain had appointed for starting had passed. Beatrice began to fancy they must intend to remain at Gibraltar, when she caught sight of another boat at a considerable distance, apparently steering for the vessel. The day had now become hazy, and she could not distinguish the figures in the boat till it drew much nearer. She began to feel half nervous about the fate of the passengers, when she heard the strange puffings and snortings from the engine, which indicated that it was getting up its steam.

The little boat, however, pushed bravely on, and at last, just as the steamer was giving one or two preparatory heaves, it was rowed close under the sides. Beatrice had already recognised the party she had seen in the morning, and she waited anxiously the appearance of the red pug-gree above the bulwarks, to see if the wearer really were her old acquaintance, Captain Denbigh.

The five ascended the steps in turn, the ladies nervously laughing and talking, having evidently been afraid of being too late—the gentlemen looking at their watches, and trying to appear innocent. The words, "The captain said four o'clock, not a second earlier, and it still wants two minutes by my watch," were said in Captain Denbigh's voice, and Captain Denbigh's eyes looked out, under the red-turbaned hat, as he passed the corner where Beatrice was sitting. He turned quickly to her—

" Miss Clyde ! "

" Captain Denbigh ! "

followed in quick succession, and then a number of other interrogatories.

If Beatrice had been inclined to feel a little awkwardness in meeting Captain Denbigh, his manner put her at ease at once—he was cordial, friendly, radiant with pleasure at meeting her, and nothing of the old lover remained about him. Indeed, after a few sentences, the announcement conveyed in the words, " I must introduce you to my wife when we go down to dinner," uttered in a rather exultant tone, effectually showed that his old *tendresse* for Beatrice had worn out.

" You are married—I must congratulate you—I am so glad!" said Beatrice, with unfeigned satisfaction.

"Yes; I was married a year ago to the daughter of my commanding officer—quite an old married man, you see—we are going home now on sick leave. You look surprised, but I really was a wretched object when we started—pulled down with jungle fever."

"Have you been on service, then?"

"A little—not much—plenty of marching, however. But we must talk afterwards—I am so glad we have met—goodbye till dinner."

And Captain Denbigh rushed downstairs to look after his wife.

A few more convulsive heaves, and an extra scream from the engine, and the vessel was fairly off, steaming towards England.

Beatrice left the deck, and went to join her mother, and tell her of the meeting with Captain Denbigh.

In less than an hour, the passengers were seated at dinner; but the Clydes were not near the Denbighs, who, having come all the way from Alexandria, were seated

amongst their Indian friends near the head
of the table. The Clydes, as new-comers,
had to find seats where they could; but
Beatrice, from her place, was able to see
Mrs. Denbigh quite well enough to form
an opinion of her appearance and manner.
She was very young-looking, small, and
fair, and had, apparently, not been long
enough in India to lose her delicate fresh-
ness of complexion. She had an abundance
of light hair, smoothly parting over a clear,
open brow, and gleaming through the
meshes of a black chenille net.

Her features were decidedly pretty, and
she had an air of good style and fashion
about her; her manner seemed quiet and
lady-like, but there was much vivacity in
her bright blue eyes, and a good deal of fun
and mischief lurking about the corners of
her mouth. Captain Denbigh was evidently
extremely devoted to her, and he looked
towards Beatrice with a sort of pride, as if
to say,

"Admire my choice."

Men who have been rejected after considerable encouragement do not always
meet an old love with the cordiality Captain
Denbigh showed to Beatrice; and perhaps,
had he not possessed a charming wife, he
might not have appeared so forgetting and
forgiving. As it was, he could admire
Beatrice without bitterness, and at the same
time say to himself that his own little wife,
younger by some years than his former
enchantress, and quite perfect in her own
style, was far the best suited to him of the
two.

"She is very nice-looking," said Mrs.
Clyde, in a low tone, to Beatrice, after
studying Mrs. Denbigh for some time;
"Poor young man! I am glad he is married, and he looks very happy. But what
a beard, to be sure!—and his face is much
darker than it used to be!"

"No wonder, mamma, particularly after
a sea voyage."

"How very odd to meet them here!" pursued Mrs. Clyde; "it will be pleasant enough, if only I keep tolerably well."

"There is every prospect of a calm passage," said Mr. Clyde. "I think you said so," turning to an officer of the ship.

"Through the dreadful Bay of Biscay?" asked Mrs. Clyde, anxiously.

"The Bay has got a bad name," said the officer. "I assure you I have often come across when it has been as calm as a millpond; and at this season of the year, I don't think we need anticipate anything else."

The prophecy proved correct, and the passage was both calm and pleasant. On the first evening, Captain Denbigh introduced his wife to the Clydes, and she and Beatrice soon became friendly; if her husband had told her the story of his former love, she had certainly received the confidence like a wise woman, for no trifling jealousy or suspicious glance betrayed that she knew he and Beatrice had ever been more than friends. Beatrice discovered one day accidentally that Captain Denbigh knew the history of the last few years of her life; and it did not appear that he considered her singular experiences implied anything to her discredit. Probably the knowledge of them solved many a puzzle in his own mind, as to the cause of her behaviour to him, and gave an interpretation to some mysterious words she had used in rejecting him.

Beatrice was greatly admired by the Indian passengers, and soon well known amongst the Denbighs' friends; she became quite a favourite on board, for now that she was happy, the true sweetness of her nature appeared, and the many gifts she possessed had free, full play, without any dash of bitterness to spoil them. No one could be a pleasanter companion—few could be more helpful and cheerful under the little difficulties and emergencies that will arise sometimes, when people are far from their homes and their accustomed requirements; and none had more resources than she to wile away the monotony of a sea voyage.

But though blithe, agreeable, and amiable, ever ready to be sociable when required, Beatrice spent many a quiet half hour of abstracted thought. Her near approach to England made her think much of Lionel, of when and where she should see him, and what would be the result.

A crowd of mingled sensations almost took away her breath when these ideas presented themselves to her mind: the remembrance of that last evening in the drawing-room at the Palace—the last glance from his eyes—the last pressure of his hand!—she could imagine she felt it yet, and a delicious thrill ran through her veins at the bare imagination.

Southampton was reached at last. On a clear spring morning the passengers landed, and the Clydes, parting from their Indian friends, and leaving Captain Denbigh struggling through the Custom House, and obtaining a promise from him and his wife of a speedy visit, hurried up to London by the first train, and were soon established in their old lodgings at Kensington.

Mrs. Clyde had taken a great fancy to Mrs. Denbigh, whose taste in dress she admired, and was really sorry at the separation; but she consoled herself by making plans for receiving her and Captain Denbigh as soon as Mr. Clyde had taken a house, which he wished to do on the Devonshire coast.

On the afternoon of Beatrice's arrival at Kensington, as she was sitting in her own room, after leaving her mother comfortably engaged with Larkins in a discussion upon the alterations that would be required in her wardrobe, now she had returned to civilized life, a message was brought to her that a gentleman was below, and wished to see her. No name was given, and Beatrice could only think of one person.

Stopping for one moment to smooth her hair, and casting at the glass a glance of such anxiety as she had seldom cast there before—fancying for an instant that she looked old and worn, and then laughing scornfully at herself for caring, she hastened down-stairs.

Lionel was standing with his face to the window when she entered the room ; but he turned round as the door closed, and, advancing, seized her hand, and held it long pressed in his.

For a minute or two neither spoke. Beatrice sat down on a couch, and Lionel placed himself by her. He looked tenderly and earnestly at her, and her eyes fell with a sweet, conscious look, and her face flushed. There was altogether a girlish timidity about her manner, that was new and captivating.

" Beatrice, you have not forgotten me all

this weary time?" said Lionel at length, almost in a whisper.

"No, indeed," said Beatrice, softly, "how could I? You saved me from misery."

"Half selfishly, 1 fear," said Lionel. " I tried to be disinterested ; but some hope of a great reward would flit before me. You would not let me speak before, and perhaps you were right. But now surely a long enough time has passed. Beatrice, I may tell you my love now ?"

His voice had gradually become more thrilling in its earnestness, and, at the last words, rose to passion.

" You are not shaken ?" said Beatrice. " You still think you are justified in loving one who has gone through what I have done? Oh! I used to scorn the world's judgment ; but now I feel what it is to bear —not for myself, but for you——"

" Beatrice !—my love !—my darling !— what need to trouble ourselves about the world's judgment? No one can really

speak ill of you. As to what is left unexplained in your former history, we can bear
misconstruction and conjectures. I care
not what is said. You are more to me than
the world; and surely we have both suffered
too much from real sorrow, to raise scruples
and shadows in the way of our happiness
now. But perhaps I have been deceiving
myself? Perhaps it would not be happiness
to you to be my wife?"

"How can you speak so?" said Beatrice,
raising her head, and looking full upon him
with the eyes he had read only too truly in
days of old. "You know—you must know
—that I——" she hesitated.

Lionel caught her in his arms, clasping
her for the first time in a wild, passionate
embrace, whilst their lips met in a long,
close kiss of unutterable love.

That moment of full life, intense bliss,
was worth years of agony, and gloomy,
lonely, death-like existence. Beatrice felt
a joy revive within her heart, that had

seemed dead since the days of earliest girlhood, and hope, that long-suffering might
well have quenched, rose buoyant in her
soul.   She would be Lionel's—Lionel would
be hers—till death should them part; and
earth would be a paradise beneath their feet.

There might be sorrow in their lives, but
none that could divide them.   They would
be one, and together brave every difficulty,
conquer in every struggle.

But whilst she yet clung to him in this
mood of high-pitched rapture and dazzling
hope, a sudden fear smote her.   Raising
herself gently out of his arms, she said :

"Your mother !—she disapproves me, I
am sure.   She will never receive me as a
daughter ?"

"She will!—she will love you when she
knows all."

"Does she know ? "

"That I love you ?—yes, I have told
her."

"But she is prejudiced against me," said

Beatrice, in a depressed tone. " I know she thinks me wild and strange."

" I own she *is* prejudiced; but her prejudices are yielding, and when she knows you love me they will quite vanish."

And Lionel again and again kissed his treasure, won at last, as if he needed each moment to assure himself that he was under no delusion.

There was not much conversation after this, but a long, happy silence, only interrupted by Mr. Clyde coming into the room. He quickly understood the state of affairs, and soon went away to summon Mrs. Clyde, who entered, smiling and gracious, quite ready to welcome a handsome man like Lionel as a son-in-law. He stayed dinner, of course; and in the evening he and Beatrice had a few quiet moments together again.

They were more serious now, and reviewed solemnly and tenderly the course of their lives, the strange position of Beatrice when they had first met, and the train of circum-

stances that had at last brought them together. Beatrice tried hard to explain to
Lionel the state of feeling that had influenced
her manner and conduct in the early days
of their acquaintance.

" It was wicked and wrong to feel as I
did," she said. " I never submitted properly
to my destiny, but fretted against it. I do
not deserve so much happiness as I have
now. Perhaps I shall bear prosperity better
than I did adversity."

" You will always be true and noble," said
Lionel, with loving flattery.

" Do not praise me so," implored Beatrice.
" I know that I have many faults, but I am
too apt to forget them, and entrench myself in pride. You must help me to discover
them and cure them—I shall trust to you
for that, as for everything else."

" My Beatrice, we will help each other,
and, if possible, my love shall secure your
happiness. I will try to make your life so
joyous, that all past misery shall only seem
a wretched dream."

" If others would also forget," began
Beatrice.

" Now, Beatrice, you will make me angry
with you.   You spoke just now of your
faults; why not receive this little cross—
the being talked about, or whatever it is—
as the punishment you think you deserve ?"

" I will look upon it so," said Beatrice,
with a sweet humility, singularly charming
in her, and almost touching, from being unexpected in one of her character and usual
demeanour.

Lionel looked at her with deep tenderness
—there was a parting embrace, and he left
the house.

The next evening he arrived at the
Laurels, and had a long conversation with
his mother after Amy had gone to bed.
Mrs. Constable had never heard a complete
history of Beatrice's life before; and, as was
natural enough in a person of her disposition, she had conceived a considerable pre-
judice against her from the circumstances

she did know.   Lionel now related the true story of the false marriage, giving, though without specifying Mr. Clyde's actual fault, the reason of her being drawn into so strange a connection; and explaining other matters which had been left obscure in the newspaper report.

Mrs. Constable listened wonderingly, and said at last,

"Well, I should have preferred your marrying a person who had been less conspicuous, but I cannot believe you would choose unwisely.   There must be virtues in Miss Clyde which I cannot see, and I know she is charming."

"It is rather cold praise, mother," said Lionel, in a mortified tone; "your taste and mine must be very different.   I could not, even to please you, force myself to like a girl like Dora Lyttelton.   No: Beatrice must be my wife.   I trust you will welcome her as a daughter; but whatever you do, we cannot give each other up.   We have known too much suffering to cast each other lightly off, when the way seems clear."

"My dear Lionel, I cannot, I do not wish to prevent you, and I will behave to Beatrice, when she is your wife, in a fitting manner. It is too much to ask me to receive her with delight, when she is altogether so un-like the woman I could have wished to be your wife. Don't look impatient—I am not meaning any particular person—certainly not Dora Lyttelton. I am convinced she would never have suited you, and I do not like her myself so well as I did. I can see that she is uncharitable and envious, and I really believe giddy little Jessie has the best heart of the two."

"Well, I suppose I must be satisfied," said Lionel; "and I am sure, when you consider all that Beatrice has gone through, when you remember how patiently we have waited, in order not to shock the world, and also to satisfy her own womanly scruples, you will think more gently of her. She owns, mother, that she loves your son dearly —you will love her for that."

Lionel was half kneeling on the ground, and his face looked so much as it had done when he was a little child, and wanted to coax something out of her, that Mrs. Constable could only draw to her the manly head lifted in loving, half-arch appeal; whilst, fondling gently the crisp, close curls clustering round it, she said, stopping in her speech to kiss the massive brow,

"My dear, foolish boy! you make your old mother do as you like—I will learn to love your Beatrice—indeed, I have been very near doing it, once or twice—but you must not be unreasonable about an old woman's fancies. One thing puzzles me," she added, after a short interval; "you used to be so fond of quoting those ridiculous lines of yours, about not minding other people's business, yet you seem to have troubled yourself a good deal about Miss Clyde's, at a time when you could not have hoped she would be anything to you. I suppose you had forgotten your theory."

"No, mother—it is a good theory, and I have always tried to reduce it to practice. But still the lines don't contain the whole truth; and when I troubled myself about Miss Clyde's business, it had already become mine. I saw she was unhappy under her engagement—you remember that afternoon of the cricket-match?—you saw it then yourself, mother—and it became my business to find out hers, and see if it could not be mended."

"Ah, Lionel! you are a true lawyer," said Mrs. Constable, shaking her head; "now, light my candle, and we will say good night."

CHAPTER XI.

WHAT THE WORLD SAID.

It was a delicious evening at the end of May, when Mrs. Constable and Amy arrived at the end of a rather long and tiresome journey. Their destination was a station not many miles from the southern coast of Devonshire; here they found a carriage waiting to convey them to the new home of the Clydes', a charming little place embosomed in trees and shrubs, which continued almost to the edge of the sea. Mrs. Constable was grave and silent; it had cost her a hard struggle to reconcile herself to the idea of receiving Beatrice as her

daughter, and she could not make up her
mind to adopt her most cordial, motherly
manner, though she fully acknowledged
that Lionel had a right to choose for himself.
Amy was silent too, wondering how she
and Beatrice would meet, after so long a
separation, and pondering upon the singularity of the circumstance that she was once
more engaged to act as Beatrice's brides-
maid.

But this wedding, she knew, would not in
the least resemble the one which was to
have taken place two years and a half ago
—all the grandeur and display which were
to have distinguished that were to be absent
from this. Beatrice had steadily resisted
every attempt of her mother's to make her
submit to the *éclat* of a splendid marriage
—she resolved not to draw upon herself
more notice than was absolutely necessary.

The road led through lovely scenery,
thickly wooded, and broken up into irregularities, jagged red cliffs rising amidst the

dense foliage, and deep, romantic glens opening out at intervals on each side. The grounds were reached at length, and Amy was silent no longer, roused into admiration of the myrtle thickets and luxuriant flowering shrubs.

But Mrs. Constable made no responding remarks; she was almost nervous at the idea of meeting Beatrice—feeling that she could not appear so kind as Lionel would wish her to be.

She need not have been afraid; the moment she saw Beatrice's face, kindling with an expression she had never seen on it before—bright, yet timid—younger, happier than it had looked three years ago—her heart warmed towards her, and she bestowed upon her a kiss of true welcome and affection. A few days passed pleasantly, though quietly. Mrs. Constable watched Beatrice in her home; saw her behaviour towards her father and mother; her gentleness, tenderness, and energy; and arrived at the conclusion, that so good a daughter must make a good wife.

Mr. Clyde, though greatly altered in externals during the last few years, had improved in some respects. He still bore the memory of past sorrows, and still more of past misdeeds, but a weight of care had been lifted from his soul, and he had lost the fitful gloom that, at times, had marked his manner. He was an agreeable, attentive host, and his old-fashioned courtesy did much towards winning Mrs. Constable's favour. Mrs. Clyde was wonderfully well; she grumbled very little at Beatrice; indeed, she was too much impressed by the magnitude of the difficulties her daughter had gone through, to dare to worry her about trifles as much as formerly. She was delighted at meeting Amy again, and she hoped to keep her and Mrs. Constable after the wedding, until the Denbighs should be able to pay her a visit; so that the prospect of being left without Beatrice did not affect her so much as it would otherwise have done.

"You must be satisfied now, my Beatrice," said Lionel, as they were walking together by the sea-shore. It was the evening before the wedding, and he had only arrived that day, so this was their first undisturbed talk. "My mother really loves you, and shows it."

"I am satisfied," said Beatrice, "and happier than I ever dreamed of being."

"And what am I?" asked Lionel, looking at her with that deep, tender gaze, that few would have expected to see in eyes so quick, piercing, and mirthful as his. "But we ought to be happier than other people, for not many have risen from such depths."

"No," said Beatrice, thoughtfully; "do you know, Lionel, it often seems to me that if I had heard my own history related as having belonged to some one else, I should think that imaginary person could never be

happy again—never forget; and yet the
eight years of blank depression first, and
acute agony afterwards—all I endured from
that man, and the terrible exposure at the
end—seem to have faded from my mind. I
feel younger than I did at seventeen, and as
happy as a bird—I could sing aloud for joy
sometimes when I wake in the morning,
and I am often afraid of being quite wild
and childish."

"You have a wonderful spring in your
nature," said Lionel; "you *must* have had,
to have borne up as you always did. My
darling! nothing, so far as I can help it,
shall quench your spirit in future. We
shall neither of us fret ourselves about little
cares—we have known agonies too great for
that. And what trouble can seem anything
to us now? Nothing can to me whilst you
are with me."

And Lionel drew her tenderly towards
him, and kissed her. So, in the darkening
twilight, they walked, almost silently, home-

wards, through the woods, on the last evening of their parted lives.

On the 2nd of June there was a dinner-
party at Wynthorpe House. The usual
country circle was assembled, but two years
and a half had not passed without bringing
some changes.

The 121st regiment had long since given
place to another at Railton, but two of the
officers happened to be present this evening
—Colonel Morley, who was staying at the
Carletons, and Mr. Curzon, whose flirtation
with Jessie Lyttelton had ended in an actual
engagement, and who was paying her one
of his periodical visits.

He would probably pay many before he
could carry her off with him, for he had not
much present wealth; but his family was
good, and he had expectations, and Jessie
was really attached to him, so Mr. Lyttelton had not objected to the engagement.

Dora, who had long had hopes of ultimately captivating Lionel Constable, had been bitterly mortified on hearing that he really was going to marry Beatrice Clyde, whom she had imagined entirely forgotten. She was rather indignant with Jessie for being engaged, and gave vent to occasional wise maxims about imprudent marriages, and rash, fancied attachments.

When the gentlemen had returned to the drawing-room, Mr. Lyttelton suddenly rang the bell, and sent for the *Times*.

"I have just remembered something I saw before dinner," he said, "which I think you will all like to hear. Ah! here it is," he added, as the paper was brought to him, and he read aloud :

"On Wednesday, the 1st inst., at the church of St. Winifred, Charlecote, Devon, by the Rev. Walter Thornton, Lionel Constable, Esq., barrister-at-law, to Beatrice, only daughter of Arthur Clyde, Esq., of Tregonall House, Charlecote."

"So they are married, after all!" said

Mrs. Lyttelton; "well, I am sure, I hope they will be happy. Lionel Constable deserves a good wife, and I daresay Miss Clyde will make one. She has had enough trouble to sober her."

"But it is a dreadful thing!" said Mrs. Carleton. "I should think a man could never forget that his wife had gone through an affair of the kind, and I should always be afraid of that Mr. Menteith turning up again."

"But even if he did, it would not signify," said Mrs. Newton. "The marriage was quite false, you know. Though it is a dreadful thing, certainly, for a young person's name to have appeared in the papers, as Miss Clyde's did. Still, one cannot wonder at Mr. Lionel's choice, for she was a very fine-looking young woman, and altogether so talented."

"I am truly delighted," said Mr. Carleton. "I always thought that those two were admirably suited to each other, and they deserved to find each other at last."

"Well, Mr. Constable must have been greatly touched," said Colonel Morley. "I know many men would have hesitated before proposing to a girl situated like Miss Clyde."

"She will have a large fortune, I should think," said Dora. "They always lived in very good style."

"It was such constancy," said Jessie. "I quite admire him for it."

"So Miss Clyde will not have the fate I once wished her, Miss Jessie?" said Colonel Morley. "Her flirtations have come to an end—Mr. Constable is not the sort of man to stand a flirting wife."

"Oh! Colonel Morley!" said Dora. "Of course no one imagines that a lady will flirt after she is married. We are not so uncharitable."

"Nor am I?" returned Colonel Morley. "I am sure I have always defended Miss Clyde as much as any one. I am only sorry that there will be no room for further conjectures about her."

"Indeed, I think there is plenty of room for conjectures," said Mrs. Carleton. "Many things are left unexplained. What made her consent to marry Mr. Menteith? Did she ever love him?"

"Love him? No, indeed!" said Mr. Carleton. "No one could look at the two together and imagine such a thing possible. Depend upon it, that was not the cause."

"Does any one know," said Colonel Morley, "what has become of that man who lectured at Railton, and claimed acquaintance with Mr. Menteith?"

"I was asking Headley about him the other day," said Mr. Carleton, "and he told me he had just had a letter from him. He is in Iceland, having gone there with a view of getting up a company to form a railway there. He says there is the finest possible opening for speculation, and that a line to the Geysers would be tremendously profitable, on account of the number of excursionists who would travel upon it."

Everyone laughed.

"What an insane idea! Quite novel and original, like the man," said Colonel Morley.

"Fancy an excursion to the Geysers!" whispered Mr. Curzon to Jessie; "suppose we go there for our honeymoon."

"We will talk of it when the railway is completed," she answered.

"Do you know that Denbigh met Miss Clyde at Gibraltar?" said Mr. Curzon, "and they came to England in the same steamer."

"Captain Denbigh is married, is he not?" asked Mrs. Carleton.

"Yes, and he has got a very nice wife, I hear," said Colonel Morley; "but what does he say, Curzon, about his old love?"

"Oh! that she is as handsome as ever, and far more generally agreeable."

"She will be spoilt, then," said Colonel Morley; "the piquancy will be gone. She must have always kept her adorers in such a pleasing state of uncertainty as to what would come next. However, I dare say, in a wife, something less exciting is preferable."

"I should like to see Denbigh again," said Fred Lyttelton; "but I can't think of him as married to any one else, when one remembers how he used to spoon Miss Clyde, you know."

"And other people used to spoon a little too, as you call it, eh, Fred?" said Mr. Newton; "and yet they have survived her loss."

"Well, I don't mind," said Fred, "you may all chaff as you like, but I say still, as I said then, that Miss Clyde was a sort of girl you don't often see; and we have not seen one like her, nor shall do, in this neighbourhood, in a hurry."

"Bravo, Fred! stand up for old friends," said Mr. Newton; "she used to behave pretty well to you, I believe."

"I am sure," observed Dora to Mrs.

Carleton, " it must be dreadful to be talked about in this way. I cannot think that any admiration a woman may receive can make up for the sacrifice of a retired, unobtrusive position."

" Oh ! Miss Clyde will not mind how much is said of her," said Mrs. Carleton, " so long as she has a few ardent partisans to stand up for her. Besides, she does not know all that is said. The only thing that surprises me is that Mrs. Constable has consented so graciously, and gone to the wedding. I am sure I have often heard her say she did not think Miss Clyde a good companion for Amy; and I know how she dislikes having anything to do with people who make themselves conspicuous."

" Mr. Constable is the person to care most for that," said Colonel Morley; " I know nothing about it, of course, but it seems to me that it would be rather unpleasant to have one's wife's qualities and actions criticized and canvassed in the way that we are now doing Mrs. Lionel Constable's."

"Oh! Lionel will not care a straw for that," said Mr. Carleton; "he would meet any hint of this kind, any doubt as to the wisdom of his choice, with his most cheery smile, and repeat, in his most careless tone, that favourite line of his, which he picked up I don't know where, and which certainly deserves to be written in characters of gold:

'Is it anybody's business what another person's is?'"

THE END.

R. BORN, PRINTER, GLOUCESTER STREET, REGENT'S PARK.

www.ingramcontent.com/pod-product-compliance
Lightning Source LLC
Chambersburg PA
CBHW020936030726
47496CB00005B/1222